W9-DGA-639

"Avram, Avram." The man whispered so as not to disturb the bar mitzvah ceremony too much.

"Mishkin's killing himself again."

"Tell him I'll be there in a minute," the rabbi replied.

"A minute's too late. He'll be finished hanging by then."

"You're a man, amen." Avram blessed the boy quickly, then raced to the hold of the ship, where a frantic crowd had gathered to try to foil Mishkin's third attempt at suicide.

"Let me die!" Mishkin screamed. "My old mother is dead. I'm all alone. I can't live without her."

"Mishkin," Avram said, struggling with the man while the ship tossed and rolled. "The Talmud says, 'If a man cries out three times for help, it shall not be denied to him a fourth.'"

"Then let me die in peace!" Mishkin proclaimed.

"So be it," the rabbi intoned. "Throw him in the ocean!"

"Wait," cried Mishkin, as several of the men started forward. "The water is cold." He hunched up his shoulders. "And, uh, I can't swim."

Avram's eyes widened. "Then you don't really want to die. Come on, say it. It's no crime."

Mishkin hesitated briefly. Then, flinging his arms to the ceiling, he shouted, "All right. I want to live!"

Some hours later, a learned woman questioned the rabbi. "I've read the Talmud," she said, "and never have I seen the principle you cited. Which book is it in?"

"Maybe it's not even there," Avram said quietly. "But you do remember, don't you—'give every man the benefit of the doubt' and 'all's well that ends well'?"

ATTENTION: SCHOOLS AND CORPORATIONS

WARNER books are available at quantity discounts with bulk purchase for educational, business, or sales promotional use. For information, please write to: SPECIAL SALES DEPARTMENT, WARNER BOOKS, 75 ROCKEFELLER PLAZA, NEW YORK, N.Y. 10019

**ARE THERE WARNER BOOKS
YOU WANT BUT CANNOT FIND IN YOUR LOCAL STORES?**

You can get any WARNER BOOKS title in print. Simply send title and retail price, plus 50¢ per order and 10¢ per copy to cover mailing and handling costs for each book desired. New York State and California residents add applicable sales tax. Enclose check or money order only, no cash please, to: WARNER BOOKS, P.O. BOX 690, NEW YORK, N.Y. 10019

THE FRISCO KID

A novelization by
Robert Grossbach

Based on a screenplay by
Michael Elias and Frank Shaw

WARNER BOOKS

A Warner Communications Company

WARNER BOOKS EDITION

Copyright © 1979 by Michael Elias and Frank Shaw
All rights reserved

ISBN 0-446-90205-5

Warner Books, Inc., 75 Rockefeller Plaza, New York, N.Y. 10019

Ⓦ A Warner Communications Company

Printed in the United States of America

First Printing: July, 1979

10 9 8 7 6 5 4 3 2 1

For Hayes Jacobs,
teacher and friend

(1)

In December, 1849, ten men with long beards, flowing black caftans, curly sideburns, wide black hats, pale skins and soft hands met in a room in the town of Kolomyja and argued like crazy. The men thought of themselves as 99.9 percent Jewish and .1 percent Polish, although they would have identified their country as Galicia, which was then part of Austria (and which is now in the Ukraine). The people at that time and in that place were accustomed to governmental confusion. Every ten or fifteen years the big powers, Prussia, Russia and Austria, having nothing better to do, carved up Eastern Europe north of the Ottoman Empire in a totally arbitrary and irrational way that guaranteed continued uprisings, repressions and further carvings.

The men in the room in Kolomyja were not concerned with such things; those were matters best left to the *goyim*. The Gentiles, after all, were occupied principally with matters of the flesh, with drinking and fighting and extensive sexual congress, whereas the Jews were creatures of the spirit. Jews were meant to study the Torah and the Talmud, to be disciplined in their thinking, ascetic in their habits, and to live a life of piety. As a result, it was not uncommon in Galicia for thousands of Jews to starve to death yearly.

The ten Jews who were arguing in Kolomyja were all rabbis, as was the eleventh person in the room, a very elderly man, who simply watched without participating, and after a while signaled with one finger to a small boy who sat on a stool in the corner. The boy quickly approached and the old man leaned down and whispered in his ear in Yiddish.

"You know where Avram is now?"

"Yes, rabbi," answered the boy.

"Go and get him."

The boy dashed from the room and the head rabbi returned his attention to the dispute.

"I don't see why they need to get someone from eight thousand miles away," one man was saying. "That, to me, is ridiculous."

"It's not ridiculous," said another. "It's an honor. It's a miraculous honor. Which is why we should send our best, not our worst."

"He's not our worst," said a third man. "There's one lower than he."

"Best, worse—all beside the point," said a fourth rabbi. "The trick is to send someone who'll get there." His face became florid and his voice rose. "It's crazy there, I hear. Wild. Savages with knives and red skins roam up and down the countryside robbing, pillaging, raping and killing. Who among us is prepared to face that?"

"Who?" said a fifth man. "All of us. What's the matter—you never heard from Cossacks? Who here doesn't have a parent or grandparent abused by Cossacks? Raise hands."

One hand went up.

"It's not the same," insisted the fourth rabbi. "Even the *goyim* there are crazy. The nobility are called cowboys and ride around singing and looping ropes. Besides, this place, this Yerba Buena, why does it need a rabbi so badly? The whole population is five hundred people from what I hear. So maybe ten of them are Jewish? Twenty?"

At this the old rabbi held up a hand. "They have recently discovered gold there. The population is going up rapidly." He paused. "Besides, what does it matter whether there are three Jews or three thousand? Someone is needed to teach."

And at this the ten men fell momentarily silent, not because they agreed—ten Jews never agree about anything—but because the head rabbi was the most learned among them and had studied at the renowned *yeshiva* in Cracow, and thus deserved respect even when he mouthed non sequiturs.

"The issue," one man said finally, "is not whether to respond—how can we refuse?—but with whom? We need someone who can command respect. Avram is a *pisher*."

"The issue *is* whether to respond," said the

rabbi who had spoken first. "You have it backwards."

And so the debate went on.

Meanwhile, outside on a frozen patch of lake, Avram Mutz, a man in his early thirties, skated in erratic, swirling patterns, his long black coat flapping in the wind. His penetrating cobalt-blue eyes were unfocused as he made his little curlicues and sudden, random stops, and he failed to notice either the light snow that was falling or the stark beauty of the winter scenery. Actually, the skating was done in time to a prayer, the Shma Yisrael, which Avram hummed to himself and to which he improvised a choreography.

"Hear, O Israel," he chanted. "The Lord our God, the Lord is One!" He leaped into the air, stumbled as he came down, and quickly regained his balance.

From a window in the synagogue, the little boy who had been sent to fetch Avram watched in fascination.

"And thou shalt love the Lord thy God with all thy heart, and with all thy soul, and with all thy might." A balletic spin, a pirouette, arms in the air.

The little boy opened the window.

"And these words, which I command thee this day, shall be upon thy heart"—a sudden race forward—"and thou shalt teach them—"

"Avram!" The voice pierced the curtain of snow. "Avram!"

Avram looked up. "A minute!" he yelled back. He did a little mincing walk, hurrying the prayer and slurring the words, but not skipping any. "—and thou shalt write them upon the door-posts of thy house and—"

"Avram, come on!"

"—upon thy gates." Avram gave a quick little nod, a final backward jump, and skated toward the synagogue.

Though a focus of community life, the synagogue was nevertheless a crude building of two stories, its wooden sides curiously skewed and uneven—the men of Kolomyja had limited tools, restricted materials and, more important, were poor craftsmen. The synagogue stood at one end of the *shtetl;* it was separated from the marketplace and business area by the rows of ramshackle, rude houses and mud streets that comprised the residential district. The market was where Jewish peddlers brought the agricultural produce of Polish, Ukranian or Austrian peasants and traded, at a small profit, for the manufactured goods of the urban middle class. Since it was where the world of the *shtetl* and the world of the *goyim* interacted, it was also where most of the "minor incidents" began—incidents that so often led to bloodbaths and massacres and pogroms.

Avram hurried up the synagogue steps, met the boy on the first floor and, still dripping wet, climbed the stairs to the head rabbi's office. As he entered, all talking came to a halt. Eleven pairs of eyes stared at him.

The boy took his place on the stool in the corner, and Avram walked to the front of the long table, the blades of his skates clomping on the floor. The silence was broken only by the sound of blood pounding through the veins in the rabbis' necks. Droplets of water ran from Avram's *peyess* down his cheeks.

"I want to talk to you in private," said the head rabbi quietly, in Yiddish.

"Yes, rebbe," said Avram. "When?"

"Now, you idiot," said the old man.

"But the other—"

"We will speak English," said the head rabbi.

Avram was one of the few students who had studied that language, primarily because he was so poor at French, German and Spanish. The older rabbis were largely unfamiliar with it, since the number of scholarly Talmudic works in English worthy of study was zero. "Remember," continued the head rabbi, "no matter what I say —don't smile."

Avram smiled.

"Look at him!" said the first rabbi. "He's grinning already! Donkey! *Nebbish!*"

"Some *schlemazel*, this one," said the second rabbi.

"Hey, *nuchshlepper!*" yelled a third. "*Trombenik!*"

There was a general outburst. Avram wiped the smile from his face. The head rabbi stood up. "SHA!" he said, raising his hands. The others quieted. The head rabbi resumed his seat and spoke softly to Avram in English.

"You have not," he said, "been a good pupil."

"I know that," said Avram, lowering his eyes. He wondered if he was about to receive a tongue-lashing of some sort, possibly have some disciplinary action taken against him.

"Out of eighty-eight students graduating from this *yeshiva*, you came in eighty-eighth."

"Uh, rebbe—"

"That is not something to boast of."

"Rebbe—"

"The others—"

"Rebbe . . ."

"What?"

"Eighty-seventh."

"Huh?"

"I was eighty-seventh, rebbe. Mendl Pincus was eighty-eighth." Thank God, Avram thought, for Mendl Pincus. Perhaps, in fact, Pincus *was* a gift from God. . . .

"So you were eighty-seventh," said the head rabbi. "So what?" He paused. "Don't smile!"

Avram, whose mouth had begun to curl into a grin, immediately made his face neutral.

"Look sad!"

Avram pulled down the corners of his mouth.

"I received this morning," said the head rabbi, "a special letter. There is a new congregation—"

"America?" blurted Avram.

"WAIT!"

The ten rabbis looked at Avram sharply.

"There is a new congregation that has no rabbi, and the parents are having great difficulties with the young people. Families—"

"I'll go!"

The head rabbi glared. "—are breaking apart. What they need is someone with a—"

"In *America* . . . ?"

"WAIT! WILL YOU WAIT!"

Avram lowered his head.

The old man took a deep breath before continuing. "They need someone with a strong will.

Not so much a scholar, but somebody with an open mind who's still capable of—"

"In America?"

"YES, IN AMERICA WOULD YOU LET ME FINISH A SENTENCE??"

Avram felt his heart about to burst in his chest.

"Some *meshuggene* has suggested your name to become the new rabbi. I discussed this with all your teachers, and your mother and your father and your grandmother."

"And they agree?"

"In the opinion of every one of them as to whether or not you could cross America and come out alive, the answer was: Never in a million years."

Avram was crestfallen.

"By law," continued the old man, "I am forced to take an official vote of the Board of Rabbis." He switched to Yiddish and addressed the assembled men. "All right, let's take a vote."

"I vote no," said the first rabbi.

"Secret ballot," said the head. "All those in favor of Avram going to America, raise your hand."

Avram looked around expectantly. Not a single arm moved, except for the small boy in the corner who waved his left hand excitedly in the air. Avram turned to him and mouthed a silent, "Thanks."

The head rabbi nodded pensively. "Close," he said. "It's a close vote. And so it falls on me to make the actual decision."

Water dripped from the brim of Avram's

hat onto the rabbi's desk. The old man positioned two ceramic ashtrays to catch the droplets.

"Sorry," said Avram.

"Stay still!" said the rabbi, repositioning the ashtrays, since Avram had moved. The next words were kindly spoken. "You . . . you're one of a kind," he said in English. "You live in your own world, but you have a good heart. And there's something else that these gentlemen don't seem to understand, and which I can't explain to them. . . . You've been touched by God."

Avram looked away, moved by these words.

"I don't know how—but I know that it's true," the old man continued.

"Thank you, rebbe."

"*And* . . . there is one more very important thing. . . ." An errant drop of water splashed from Avram's chin onto some papers. "You've studied English."

"I've done my best, rebbe."

"I know, I know." The old man pulled himself erect. "So, cowboy . . . I'm sending you to Yerba Buena."

"Where is Yerba Buena?"

"Yerba Buena is on the west coast of America." He looked down at the moist papers before him and ran his fingers over some spidery script. "Here—they changed its name recently. They now call it San Francisco."

"San Francisco," echoed Avram.

"You go by way of Philadelphia. Philadelphia, you've heard of?"

"Yes, rebbe," said Avram excitedly.

"Good." The old man switched back to Yiddish to address the group. "All right, I've decided. He goes to America."

There was pandemonium. The room was filled with outraged bellows in Yiddish, German, Polish and Russian. (Hebrew has no curse words.) Several of the rabbis left their seats and stormed up to the head rabbi's desk for a direct confrontation.

The old man leaned back in his chair, his eyes on Avram. "Go!" he yelled. "Get out quick."

Avram left as the remaining group of maddened rabbis closed in.

• • •

Avram's father was a stringy man named Simon Mutz, a tailor by trade, whose motto was "It could be worse." This, in fact, is exactly what he told his son when Avram came home with the news. "I have been doing research on America ever since I spoke with Rebbe Gittelman. It's not such a horrible place."

"But you told the rebbe you didn't think I could survive there," said Avram.

"True enough," said his father. "But what makes you think you'll survive here? Believe me, for Jews there's no place safe. The idea is to stay one step ahead of the ax."

Simon Mutz knew whereof he spoke and practiced what he preached. He had moved his family six times in the last eighteen years, shifting from Lvov to Jaroslaw to Cracow and back, before settling in Kolomyja. He had seen heads of state come and go, taxes imposed and ended only to be reimposed. He had seen residence restrictions on Jews, curtailing movement from city to city; laws forbidding Jewish artisans to work for Gentiles; taxes on synagogues, on kosher meat, even on Friday-night candles. He had seen Jews removed from inn-keeping, from selling liquor, from farming. He had seen Jews prevented from sending money to Palestine, from using documents written in Hebrew or Yiddish. But, always, even before things shifted, there were ways around.

Galicia's laws were administered unevenly and capriciously. Officials could be bribed. Kind men could be found. If necessary, fines could be paid. And, if one waited long enough, things changed. The revolution of 1848 had resulted in the special Jewish taxes being canceled. The constitution of March, 1849 conferred complete equality on Jews in Austria and made Galicia a semi-autonomous province with its own governor. Of course, sentiment was rising for a return to the old conditions, but, in the meantime, "It could be worse." The principal rule, Simon knew, was: *Keep away from the Russians.* Nicholas I was the worst kind of maniac, a stupid one. The only way to enlighten him would be to assassinate him.

About America, Simon liked what he'd read and heard. Yes, the people were rough and crude. Yes, the land was harsh, the living conditions squalid in the east, savage on the frontiers. So what else was new? But at least prejudice there was minimal. Problems were the same for everyone. Ten years earlier, in 1840, the United States had spoken out on behalf of the Jews in Damascus. There, when a number of Jewish artisans

17

had been arrested on a phony murder charge, and confessions tortured out of them, President Van Buren himself had sent a direct message to Mehemet Ali, Pasha of Egypt (which controlled Syria). The sympathies of the United States were thoroughly with the Hebrews.

"One advantage you'll have," said Simon to Avram, "and one advantage only. In America, there is no prejudice against Jews." He paused. "Why do you think this is?"

"I don't know," said Avram. "It doesn't seem reasonable."

"There is no prejudice because there are not enough of us there," said Simon. "When more come, the *goyim* will start to hate. Until then...." He shrugged.

"I hope I'm worthy of everyone's faith," said Avram.

"You're worthy," said his father. "They have no faith." He gripped Avram by the shoulders. "Don't let it worry you." He reached up to touch his son's cheek. "You'll be fine. I believe in you, and you believe in yourself. That's what counts. Whatever else happens is in the hands of God."

"I'll miss you," said Avram. And for the first time, a terrible realization struck him: He would never see his father or mother again. They would grow old and die, and he would never be able to hear their voices, hug them. He gripped his father tightly now, pressing his face into the rough cloth of the old man's vest. "I'm not sure I really want to go," he said, the tears blurring his eyes.

"You go," his father whispered. "You go. What have you got here?"

* * *

The thin December sunlight made multi-colored streamers as it filtered through the stained glass windows of the synagogue. For this particular occasion, Avram's mother, father and grandparents had been granted seats along the eastern wall, a special honor, since it was there that the Ark was located; usually only the *sheyne Yidn*, the men of learning, of substance, were permitted to stay there. Facing them, in a descending hierarchy, were the rows of burghers; the commoners, usually assumed to be ignorant, poor, or both; and finally, on the western wall, the beggars and impoverished strangers. Rabbi Gittelman stood at the pulpit, with Avram by his side. At his signal, the head of the congregation brought over a velvet satchel the size of two prayer books, which the rabbi placed in Avram's outstretched arms.

"Open it," he ordered.

Avram loosened the drawstring. Inside were two scrolls, densely covered with Hebrew writing.

"Every congregation needs a Torah," said the rabbi. "This one will be yours." He motioned again to the head of the congregation, who now brought over a second velvet bag, much smaller than the first. This one the rabbi opened himself, revealing an engraved silver plate. "And just so you don't forget, here is a copy of the Ten Commandments. It's a little lighter than the one God gave to Moses, but then you'll be traveling a little farther." He hung the plate on the handles of the Torah by a fine silver chain. "The bag I'll keep," he added.

Avram felt the blood rush to his head. He was stunned, awed. The Torah, a scroll containing the Five Books of Moses, handwritten by a scribe on parchment, was priceless beyond expression. Throughout Jewish history, it had held a sacrosanct place; innumerable martyrs had sacrificed their lives to preserve and transmit it over the generations. And the silver Ten Commandments plate was easily worth its weight in gold. I'll never make it, thought Avram. I'll disgrace myself before God. Near the Ark, he saw his father weeping.

"America is a land of dreams," said the rabbi. "It's a place to start fresh, a place where men are judged by what they do instead of the clothes they wear, or the language they speak. It is a place where Jewish learning and tradition can flourish, and where there are no czars or kings to crush us under their boots. The American president is a man called Zach Taylor, and his assistant president is Millard Fillmore. Remember those names! Someday the people of Galicia will regard them as heroes." The old man put his hand around Avram's shoulders. "And maybe you too, eh? Maybe Avram Mutz also."

Avram kissed the Torah and held it up to the Ark. He began to pray, and in the background the voices of the chorus rose. The resonant tenor of the cantor filled the room. And it came to Avram, finally, that the richness of the gifts he had received, their utter extravagance beyond the means of the poor congregation, represented an expression less of religious enthusiasm than of vicarious projection. He was living out their dreams, escaping the prison of their lives. God help him if he should disappoint them.

• • •

An emigration society in Lemberg had helped arrange Avram's route. On a cloudy day in early January, 1850, laden with tickets, instructions on tiny pieces of paper, his Torah and Commandments, a *Megillah*, a *shofar*, four prayer books, one change of clothing, and an apple, he departed by wagon for Nowy Sacz, a small *shtetl* near the Bohemian border. From Nowy Sacz, he went to Moravska-Ostrava, a city with paved streets, where he returned the wagon to a sister branch of the emigration society and caught a stagecoach for Prague. In years past such travel would have been difficult for a Jew, but 1850 was an exception. The new Hapsburg monarch, Francis Joseph I, had only been in power for a little over a year and he was treading gingerly; the revolutions of 1848 had produced a wave of democratic reforms. There was even a constitution in effect, drafted by advisors to the crown.

Avram stayed in Prague for two days, rooming in a third-class hotel halfway between Tyn Church and the Vltava River, which the city straddled. On the third day he took a ferry to Melnick, where he caught a river steamer that sailed up the Elbe. Two weeks later, the steamer deposited him and three hundred others on a dock in Hamburg. For eighteen hours the emigrants huddled miserably together, with only a few rotting wooden sheds to protect them from a cold winter rain. Then, appearing suddenly from around a bend in the river, came their transportation to America. The emigrants let out a cheer. "We're saved!" said one. "Our troubles are over."

The two-masted brig, *Colibri,* pulled up to the pier. She was a cotton ship, thirty years old, her timbers as decayed as the sheds on the wharf. The passengers walked across the creaking deck until they found the hole leading to the steerage section. "Gateway to a new life," said Avram, who had already gained much respect because of his rabbinical training. He climbed down the ladder.

The steerage section was six feet in height. Years later, occasional scholars would suggest this as an explanation of why there were so few tall Jews in America. Around the periphery ran two layers of berths, plywood platforms that slept five across. Each person was issued a towel and a bar of soap; three people shared a life preserver. The center area was reserved for hogs, cattle and hens. Barrels of drinking water were stored near one bulkhead, along with cartons of rice and potatoes. Isn't it just like our congregation, thought Avram, to book me aboard a luxury ship.

Quickly it became known that the rabbi spoke English. Eager to learn, many of the emigrants began pressing him for lessons. By the second week Avram was giving formal classes each day on deck. They were conducted near the lifeboat, which provided the groups of pale, nauseated students with some small shelter from the icy winds.

"I am *seekrank,*" said Moishe Fishbein.

"No," said Avram sharply. He consulted his grammar book. "I am seasick."

"I am *seekrank*," repeated Fishbein.

"You are sea*sick*," insisted Avram. "You understand?"

Fishbein began to retch.

"My name," called out a woman, "is Anna Lifschitz."

"Good," said Avram. He raised his hands so that the class might ask the ritual question.

"Where are you going?" said the class.

"I am seasick," said Anna Lifschitz.

"No," said Avram. "You go to Philadelphia."

"I am *seekrank*," called out Fishbein during a respite from his retching.

"You are sea*sick*," corrected Avram.

"*I* am seasick," persisted Mrs. Lifschitz.

"She is seasick," said Avram to the class.

A second man spoke up. "*I* am seasick."

"Good," said Avram.

"My name is Chaim Kugelman."

"Chaim is seasick," said Avram.

"I am see*krank*," said Fishbein.

"You are SEASICK!" said Avram, losing patience and beginning to feel nauseated himself. A spray of water washed over the deck.

A softness came into Fishbein's eyes. "I am SEA SICK!"

"Yes," said Avram, nodding. "Yes." And then as the ship swayed violently back and forth, "Oy."

The class repeated: "Oy."

"We are all seasick," said Avram, heading for the railing.

"We are all seasick," said the class.

23

(2)

In the steerage section, the bodies were squeezed together, although the people were not sleeping. Damp clothes were hung on the corner posts of the berths; both oil lamps and memorial lamps cast flickering shadows on the low ceiling. Occasionally, children cried or moaned, and were quickly silenced by a parent. In a corner, a small table cloth was spread over the top of a barrel. Avram's Torah lay open on the makeshift pulpit, while a young boy haltingly chanted a passage. Avram stood beside him, nodding from time to time, helping with a difficult word.

A figure came scrambling through the hatch from the freight compartment. "Rabbi!" he shouted.

Avram held up a hand for the man to be

quiet, then motioned for the boy to continue. It was a long Haftorah for this particular month and his voice was dry from the chanting. Drinking water had to be severely rationed; already there had been fist fights over supplies. Fish, the only fresh food available, could not be eaten because it caused thirst.

"Swallow," said Avram.

The boy resumed his reading.

The man from the freight hold pushed forward until he stood a foot away from the barrel. "It's Mishkin," he whispered loudly.

"Please," Avram whispered back. "Can't you see we have a Bar Mitzvah here?"

"He's killing himself," said the man urgently.

Avram stared at the ceiling. "Again?"

"Again."

"Tell him I'll be there in a minute."

"A minute is too late, he's strung up."

Avram exhaled sharply. "All right." He touched the young boy's *yarmulka.* "You're a man. . . . Amen. Go in good health." He followed the man back toward the freight hatch.

In the hold, Mishkin, a burly, mustachioed shoemaker of thirty-five was killing himself for the third time. Two weeks out of Hamburg his mother had died of tuberculosis and had to be buried at sea. Once a week since then Mishkin had tried to end his own life. He hung now by a rope from a crossbeam on the ceiling. The cargo hold was eight feet in height; earlier, when Mishkin had tried to hang himself in the steerage section, his feet had simply touched the floor. Two old Jewish men and an Italian woman were struggling to keep Mishkin's 240-pound body

26

aloft as the ship lurched from side to side. They strained to keep their balance while coping with Mishkin's kicking legs.

"Let me die!" he screamed. "What right have you? Let me die!"

"You *gonif*, you," shouted one of the old men. "When you pay me back my money you can die all you want. Until then, never!"

Mishkin spotted Avram. "I can't live without her!" he wailed.

"What's a matta him?" said the Italian woman, addressing Avram as she clung to Mishkin's calves. "He broke up-a with-a his girlfriend?"

"Mother," said Avram.

The woman's eyes widened. "His Mama was-a his girlfriend?"

Avram started to shake his head, but the woman seemed not to see.

"That's-a disgusting," she said, abandoning Mishkin's calves and walking off.

Avram raced forward and plunged his head between Mishkin's legs. A group of people from the congregation entered the hold, only to stumble all over themselves as the ship hit a wave. The two old men were flung to the floor, leaving Mishkin teetering on Avram's shoulders. Avram felt his knees begin to buckle. "Help," he croaked.

Several members of the congregation began creeping toward them.

"Mishkin!" said Avram. "Quick, get off!"

He felt himself collapsing under the weight, and then suddenly six pairs of hands reached up and relieved the pressure. Mishkin was held firmly aloft while the noose was removed from his neck.

"Mishkin," said Avram, "what's with you?"

"I'm all alone."

"You're not. God sees."

"I can't live without her."

"This is not the answer, Mishkin. Think how it looks."

"Why did she have to die?"

"Because she was flesh and blood, as we all are. Dying is part of life. If you don't want to die, don't live."

"She was a saint," said Mishkin.

"All right, so she was a saint."

"She was an angel. She was—"

"She was eighty-nine years old," reminded Avram.

Mishkin rubbed his throat where the rope had chafed. "I want to die," he said resolutely. He snatched the noose from the man holding it and tried to lower it over his head.

"Mishkin," said Avram, struggling with him and rolling with the motion of the ship, "it says in the Talmud—"

"Let go the rope!"

"—It says, 'If a man cries out three times for help, it shall not be denied to him a fourth.'"

"Let me die in peace!"

Avram let go the noose. "So be it."

Mishkin stared at him, the loop of rope held aloft. "Thank you, rabbi," he said.

Avram raised a hand. "But not this way. This way is a sin." He turned to the crowd of onlookers. "Throw him into the ocean."

There was a murmur from the crowd. Several of the men tentatively started forward.

"Wait!" said Mishkin. "The water is cold." He hunched up his shoulders.

"Only for a couple minutes," said Avram.

"And, uh, I can't swim."

Avram's eyes widened theatrically. "Then you don't want to die?"

"Well, I . . ."

Then you don't want to die?

Mishkin looked confused. "I . . . I . . ."

"Say it!" shouted Avram. "It's no crime. Say it, Mishkin!"

Mishkin hesitated, then raised his arms to the ceiling. "I want to *live!*" he shouted.

"Again."

"I want to live!"

The crowd cheered and surged forward. Two men lifted Avram on their shoulders as Mishkin clapped his hands together. "Life!" he yelled. "Life!" Unnoticed, the loop of rope slipped down over Avram's neck. People were pounding Mishkin on the back; several women rushed up to kiss him. At the rear, someone began to play *Hahvah Nagila* on a violin, and a group of men and women formed a circle and began to dance. "Congratulations!" people shouted, as Mishkin moved happily through the crowd.

Avram, dangling, began to choke. His face turned beet-red. His hands clawed the air trying to find the rope. Tightening his neck muscles in a final burst of energy, he squawked, "I, too, want to live!"

An old woman happened to glance around. "Oh, my God!" she shouted. "The rabbi!"

And they took Avram down just before he passed out.

• • •

It was the dinner hour. People sat on the floor around spread-out blankets. The menu for this evening was one piece of black bread, a cup of tea, and a bowl of potato soup. Avram spied an empty space next to a beautiful young woman. Although it was the custom for scholars to lead an ascetic life, devote themselves to Talmudic problems, and even to walk with downcast eyes, he could not help noticing this girl. She had full lips, almond eyes, and long, braided hair piled up on top of her head. As Avram came toward her, she moved over slightly, making the space next to her even wider. A shy smile flickered over her mouth, and Avram felt a throbbing in his neck. He thought of the picture he carried with him, the photograph of Sarah Mindl. True, Sarah had a chest like a watermelon, but the face . . . There was no comparison. Suddenly Mishkin appeared and stepped toward the place for which Avram was heading. Avram slowed, permitting Mishkin to slide in before him, and took a position at a blanket spread nearby. He sipped some tea. When he looked up, he saw the lovely young girl staring at him, but she quickly turned away. A voice next to him disturbed his thoughts.

"Sometimes in life, Rabbi, you have to be a little bold to get what you want."

Avram glanced at the elderly matron sitting next to him.

"Rachel Adler," said the woman, extending a hand.

Avram shook it. "Sometimes," he said, "I wish I could be."

"May I ask a question?"

"Of course."

"Where does it say in the Talmud that if a man cries out three times for help, it shall not be denied to him a fourth?"

"You're familiar with the Talmud?"

"I have studied fifty-six of the sixty-three books."

"And you never came across that principle?"

"Not that I remember."

"Could it be that it's in one of the sections you haven't gotten to?"

"It could," said Mrs. Adler. "This is what I'm asking."

Avram's eyes sparkled as he mumbled the blessings for bread. Then he tore off a piece of dark brown crust. "It's not," he said.

Mrs. Adler smiled.

"But there are two other Talmudic principles that I do think apply."

"Which are . . . ?"

" 'Give every man the benefit of the doubt', and 'All is well that ends well.' "

Mrs. Adler looked up at him. "I'll tell you something, Rabbi—you got possibilities."

"Thank you," said Avram. "I hope they're good ones."

Three days later it was Avram's turn for a bath. The ship had been at sea for nearly six weeks now, and head and body lice were becoming a serious problem. Sitting naked in the cut-down water barrel, Avram peeked out an opening in the makeshift curtains that surrounded it. Mishkin entered, carrying a large bucket.

"Hot water for the rabbi," he chanted, emptying the steaming bucket into the barrel.

Avram soaped himself vigorously. "This is marvelous," he said. "Where did you get it?"

"I spoke to one of the ship's officials—a mate, I think they call him," said Mishkin. "I explained to him the importance."

"A miracle," said Avram. "I'm truly grateful, Mishkin. I bet even the captain doesn't have water so hot this morning."

"That's true," said Mishkin.

Avram ran the soap over his body, feeling the bony ribs like rungs on a ladder from his chest to his hollow stomach. How subtle God was, he marveled. When there was little food to eat, He made you seasick to kill your appetite. When the bathtub was a barrel, He insured you'd be slim enough to fit comfortably inside. His hand was everywhere. Outside, Avram heard footsteps, the sound of many people running. There was excited shouting. A hand parted the curtains and a man leaned inside. "America! Rabbi, America!"

Avram stood up and said a quick prayer. America—they had made it! The man rushed off, and a moment later Mishkin followed, accidentally catching his hand in one of the blankets that shielded the bathtub, and pulling it down. Avram saw dozens of people scurrying toward the deck, thrilled to be getting the first glimpse of their new country. Excited voices filled the steerage area; women kissed their babies in delirious joy. Still, Avram observed, several in the crowd did pause long enough to stop and stare at the barrel. Because, in all the world, the only sight for a new immigrant comparable to his first view of America was the vision of a naked rabbi.

• • •

Topside, still dripping through hastily put-on clothes, Avram strained to see through the thick dawn fog. A man put his arm around Avram's shoulder and pointed into the distance.

"New York, Rabbi."

"I think this is supposed to be Philadelphia," said Avram.

"No, no, this is New York," said the man. "We're in the mouth of the Hudson River."

"Perhaps I'm misinformed," said Avram. "I thought we were going to Philadelphia."

A second man poked the first in the stomach. "Hey, you, *chacham!* What are you telling the rabbi? This is not the Hudson, this is the Delaware."

"It is?" said the first man.

"Certainly it is. You see those lights?" He pointed to some bright spots on the shore. "That's Philadelphia. Soon, the fog will lift and you'll be able to see the Statue of Liberty."

"I thought that was in New York," said the first man.

"Shows you what you don't know."

Avram, amazed, lost in thought, could only stare. "It's . . . wonderful," he mumbled to himself. "Wonderful."

Actually, the lights the immigrants had seen

were from Camden, New Jersey, across the river. It was not till nearly noon that the ship finally docked at Penn's Landing, and a gangplank was lowered into a seething array of waiting relatives, baggagemen, haulers, stevedores, pickpockets, con men, whores, ragamuffins, hawkers, vendors and militiamen. Immigration at this time was controlled by the individual states; it would be another forty years before a Supreme Court decision gave jurisdiction in this area to the federal government. The state of Pennsylvania was quite lenient. Avram, his cardboard suitcase clutched to his chest, made his way through the chaotic crowd to a row of gates, each manned by two men. The first studied him carefully and marked something on a small card.

"*Vee hayst eer?*" he said.

"Avram Mutz."

The man nodded and wrote down the name. "Speak English?" he added.

"Yes," said Avram. "Slowly."

"Ever been arrested for a crime of moral turpitude?"

Avram had no idea what the man was talking about. "No," he said.

"Country of origin?"

"What?"

"Where you from, Avram?"

"Galicia."

"Gal-i-ci-a," repeated the man, writing it on a card. "Ever have consumption, granuloma, or trachoma?"

"I don't think so," said Avram. "My family was very poor."

The man nodded and motioned to the sec-

34

ond fellow. This one looked into Avram's eyes with an instrument, then checked his ears and throat. A moment later, he nodded.

"Yer okay," said the first man, placing Avram's card in a growing pile. "Welcome to the state of Pennsylvania."

"Thank you," said Avram gratefully. "You're a nice chap." He lingered confusedly at the end of the pier until he spotted a low brick building with a sign, TICKET OFFICE, over the door. He'd just picked up his suitcase again when a voice called to him from the teeming throng.

"Rabbi! Rabbi Mutz!"

Avram turned and spotted Mishkin with the beautiful young girl he'd noticed a week earlier at dinner. As they approached, the girl smiled at Avram, a coy, seductive smile that made his heart ache.

"I like this Philadelphia," said Mishkin, raising his voice above the noise of the crowd.

"It seems like quite a city," temporized Avram.

Mishkin chuckled. "It's suffocating, it's dirty, it's crowded. I like it."

"It's just like home," said the girl. Her eyes met Avram's. "Goodbye, Rabbi."

Avram nodded. "Yes. Goodbye, Mishkin." He shrugged. "Goodbye . . . young lady."

Mishkin and the girl disappeared in the throng of immigrants. "Watch out for yourself," Mishkin called back. "There's all kinds of crazy people in this world."

It could be worse, thought Avram. He entered the low building and stood on a line that formed in front of a barred window. *Booking*

Agent, read the sign. Avram fumbled in his pocket until he found a small slip of paper. He studied it as he slowly moved up. "The President Washington to San Francisco," he whispered to himself. "One way, please." He put the paper down and repeated the message. "The President Washington to San Francisco. One way, please."

"You're going west?" said the man behind him.

"No," said Avram. "To San Francisco. One way, please."

The man shook his head as Avram reached the ticket booth.

"What can I do for you?" asked the booking agent.

Avram placed three fifty-dollar bills on the ticket counter. The emigration society had been efficient, giving him American currency in advance to avoid his being cheated by money changers. Thirty-four dollars for the passage from Hamburg, a hundred fifty for the trip around Cape Horn. "The President San Francisco to Washington," said Avram clearly. "One way, please."

"What?" said the agent.

"President San Francisco to Washington," said Avram.

"I got nothin' that moves by that name," said the man.

Avram concentrated, then smiled. "Ah, excuse please," he said sheepishly. "I meant the President Washington to San Francisco. I said it incorrectly."

The agent pushed the bills back toward Avram. "She left yesterday."

Avram nodded. "The President Washington to San Francisco," he repeated, assuming the agent wanted to start the transaction over from the beginning. "One way, please."

The agent shook his head. "Boat's gone."

"*Vus?*" said Avram.

The agent leaned closer to Avram and raised his voice, an age-old technique for communicating with those not fluent in a particular language. "*Bateau disparu*," he said.

"I'm sorry," said Avram, "I don't—"

"*Barca partito, shiff gehen!* Get it?"

Avram looked on in bewilderment as the man behind him tapped him on the shoulder.

"What did he say?"

Avram shrugged and stepped aside. The man, a pleasant-faced gentleman in his late thirties or early forties, leaned into the window. "Mister!" he said. "'Scuse me. Sir?"

"Help you?" said the agent.

"What did you just say about the ship to San Francisco?"

"Gone," said the agent. "She left yesterday."

"But that can't be."

"Saw her sail myself."

"But she's supposed to leave first tide tomorrow."

"Supposed to? What the hell's the matter with you?" said the agent. "It's the gold rush, ain't you people heard anything?"

"But the schedule—"

"There's no more schedules, no more 'supposed to's'," said the ticket agent gruffly. "Next ship is in one month."

"Oh God," said the man, his shoulders

37

slumping. "Oh God, help me. Just this morning me and my brother got the news that our Mum is dying in San Francisco." He wandered away from the booth and bent to one knee, a few feet from Avram. He buried his face in his hands. "What am I gonna do?" he cried. "What am I gonna do?"

Avram, also stunned, had already begun to recover. He had learned from experience that one should expect plans to fall through. This was the nature of the universe. What would have been absolutely amazing was if everything had gone perfectly. He leaned over the kneeling man. "Excuse me, sir, my name is Avram Mutz."

The man looked up. "Darryll Diggs," he said tearfully. "Looks like we're in the same boat. Or rather out of the same boat."

"Isn't there some other way that one could get to San Francisco?"

"Not for us, sir," said Darryll. Slowly, he pulled himself erect. "Just ten minutes ago me and my brother sold our horses and wagon so's we could purchase tickets on this here boat. Now we ain't got neither."

"A pity," said Avram.

"My Mum'll die alone now," said Darryll forlornly.

Avram thought of his own parents back in Kolomyja. "Perhaps," he said, "you can go to the man who bought your wagon and tell him your troubles."

"Awe, he won't be interested in—"

"But maybe if you give him back his money, he would return the wagon."

38

Darryll cocked his head. "You think he'll do it?"

"If he's a good man," said Avram.

Suddenly, Darryll seized Avram's arm. "Would you help me? Please, mister, I'm not much good at explainin' things. I usually just start to cry."

Avram was puzzled. "You want *me* to help *you?* I just got off the boat."

"Please," said Darryll, and his look was so sincere and ingenuous that Avram immediately made up his mind.

"I'll try," he said. "That's all I can do."

"Thank you," said Darryll, pumping Avram's hand. "Thank you, sir. You don't know what this means to me."

"I don't speak English so well," said Avram, "but I'll—"

"You speak it fine," said Darryll. "Just fine."

He led Avram out of the ticket office and down a street that ran parallel to the waterfront. Clusters of immigrants still remained on the pier, men in caps and cloth jackets, women in heavy skirts and shawls; sacks filled with pots and pans rested against the pilings. Avram took a final look at the *Colibri*, ropes crisscrossing the masts and decks like a stand of trees in winter, the *Passengers-Not-Allowed-on-Bridge* sign hanging loosely by one corner. Goodbye, he thought. It had been a terrible journey—and a wonderful one.

They threaded their way past dock workers, drunken seamen, barrels, carts, and packing crates, then turned inland down a narrow street. Avram clutched his suitcase close to his body.

"What, uh, does your mother have?" he asked Darryll tentatively.

"She got the fever," said Darryll. "Malaria. She went to California by way of the Isthmus, see, an' that's where she come down with it."

"There was no other way she could go?"

"Well, she didn't have the money for a ship around the Horn, and overland would've been just too hard. Lotta people die tryin' a get to San Francisco, starve to death, or freeze. And Mum's nearly seventy, ya know."

"Mine too," said Avram.

"You from Germany?" asked Darryll. "Lotta folks from Germany comin' in these days."

"A little farther east," said Avram. "Galicia. Part of partitioned Poland. Ruled by the Hapsburgs."

"Never heard of them," said Darryll. "You a peddler? Most people from Europe is peddlers."

"No," said Avram. "Not me."

They turned into a street lined with two- and three-story buildings, mostly brick but some wood, awnings overhanging the sidewalks, stalls with fruit, and vegetables and household appliances out in front, coaches and carts and wagons of every description clogging the unpaved gutter. Vendors, businessmen, housewives, and children wove in and out among the stands, stopping to examine or haggle or merely to pass the time.

"Looks like Cracow," said Avram.

And, in fact, many of the people did have a European appearance. A moment later, Darryll stopped in front of a livery stable. Parked on the street was a small, canvas-topped wagon with

40

two tired-looking horses. Next to the wagon was a large, muscular man wearing a derby and drooping mustache that seemed to accentuate his scowl.

"This is it," said Darryll to Avram.

"Everything go all right?" asked the scowling man.

"The boat sailed," said Darryll.

"What?"

"It sailed! It's the gold rush, Matt. Everyone's goin' crazy. The boat sailed yesterday."

An older man appeared from behind the wagon. He nodded curtly to Darryll, then moved toward one of the horses and adjusted a harness.

"What do we do now?" said the scowling man.

"God may be on our side yet, Matt," said Darryll, "thanks to this gentleman." He gently pushed Avram forward. "Avram, this is my brother, Matthew Diggs."

Matt slowly extended a callused hand.

"Avram Mutz," said Avram. "How do you do?"

Matt just squinted slightly as Darryll turned to the man near the horses. "Mr. Jones, we missed our boat and we find ourselves in a desperate state."

Jones did not turn from the traces. "Sorry to hear that," he said, his voice neutral.

"We need our horses and wagon back, please, so we can get to San Francisco to see our Mum before she dies."

Jones clicked his tongue and raised his bushy eyebrows.

"So if you'd be kind enough to take your

money back . . ." Darryll pulled a roll of bills from his pocket and thrust it in Jones's direction.

Jones made no move to accept. "I sympathize with your misfortune, fellas, but I'm in the business of buying and selling. And I don't sell unless I make a profit."

Darryll, his face anguished, whirled to face his brother. "But we don't have no money to give you a profit."

Jones shrugged. "Then we don't do no business."

Avram, suitcase between his feet, decided it was time to speak up. "Tell me, please," he said to Jones, "how much profit must you have from these people?"

Jones looked Avram up and down, then glanced back at the Diggs brothers before pursing his lips. "Oh, I'd say a hundred, maybe a hundred fifty dollars. Something like that."

Darryll shook his head. "That's it, Matt, we're sunk." He held out a hand to Avram. "Thanks for your help, Avram. I'm sorry I wasted your time." He put his hand on Matt's shoulder, and the two of them began to walk away.

"Wait," said Avram. He looked up at Jones. "Perhaps, sir, in view of the circumstances, you might consider something less. Say . . . thirty dollars. If you would take thirty, I would pay you myself."

The Diggs brothers stopped in their tracks.

"For thirty you get spit," said Jones.

Avram did not know what "spit" meant, but thought it was a start. "I know it's not much," he said, "but payment would be immediate, and

42

you'd have the satisfaction of having performed a service for humanity."

Jones looked away. "Seventy-five is the lowest I could go."

Avram removed a bill from the purse he kept in his coat. "I could give you fifty right now. The rest of the money for my passage I must return to the emigration society that helped me." He dangled the fifty in front of Jones's face.

Jones paused a moment, then reached up and snatched the bill.

Darryll and Matt had moved back close to the horses. Darryll shook his head. "That's kind of you, Avram, but I don't know how we could ever pay you back. Maybe you'd better—"

Avram held up a hand. His eyes sparkled. "If you could find a seat on your wagon to San Francisco, I would be more than repaid."

Darryll's face wrinkled in a smile. "You pay fifty dollars, you can have the seat with the cushion. Can't he, Matt?"

"All the way," said Matt.

"I'll share the cushion," said Avram.

Jones headed back into the livery. "Wagon's yours," he said over his shoulder.

"Yowee!" shouted Darryll. He rushed forward and hugged Avram in his arms. "Matt, the Lord has smiled on you an' me today."

Avram grinned. "All of us," he said, marveling at his good fortune.

43

(3)

In 1846, the white population of Yerba Buena was seven hundred (half of them American), with 150 residents of other races. Three years later, forty thousand people arrived by sea and an equal number by land across the Great Basin, or north, from Mexico. All this, of course, because eons before, in the upheavals that formed the Sierras, a long band of volcanic rock had been disgorged from the bowels of the earth, and in that rock were streaks and seams of pure, metallic gold. Centuries of erosion had loosened flakes and nuggets of the soft, yellow substance and conveniently deposited them in backwaters and gravel beds from the Mariposa River to the Feather, from the Calaveras to the Yuba. On January 28, 1848, James W.

Marshall walked into Sutter's Fort near Sacramento with a white cotton handkerchief, carefully formed into a small sack. . . .

The Benders had come early to San Francisco and had no interest in prospecting. They arrived in October of 1848, and correctly anticipated what would happen: Everyone but the miners would get rich. The Benders were a family of traders who'd settled in Salem, Oregon in 1843, and as soon as news of the gold discovery became known they'd headed south with their wagons of goods, stopping at various forts on the way and following a route very similar to the one Charles Wilkes had pioneered seven years earlier. The days spent at the forts provided a dual function. They served as safe havens from the Umpqua Indians, bands of whom were still marauding in the region, and they provided useful trading opportunities for the Benders to exchange the pelts they'd bought from Oregon trappers for the cooking utensils and domestic goods they forsaw would be needed in San Francisco.

In May of 1849, the family already owned five separate stores, two hotels and a warehouse. This, when new arrivals were forced to live in tents and cook meals over campfires, when shiploads of goods were dumped on the beach for lack of storage space, when abandoned ships—their crews run off to go prospecting—were simply drawn up on the mud and used for housing or shops. Eggs sold for a dollar each, porters charged two dollars a bag, a drink of whiskey cost a pinch of gold dust. There was gambling and fighting, raping and whoring, murder and hanging. The Benders avoided craziness and became wealthy. The money poured in no matter what they did, effortlessly and sinfully, copiously, embarrassingly. Life was too good, it couldn't last. Naturally, they turned to God.

Samuel Bender sat in his favorite reclining chair in the living room. Around him was a cacophony of Yiddish, Polish, Russian, German and English, all spoken by the ten percent representation of the Jewish community of San Francisco: twelve people. A thin, balding man named Isaac Bialik separated himself from the crowd.

"Gentlemen, if you please, we should begin."

The talking continued.

"Gentlemen," repeated Bialik. "Please. A little quiet."

The noise died down. Bender remained silent. He watched as his oldest daughter, Sarah Mindl, walked around with the tray of teacups. Sarah Mindl had stringy hair, a pointy nose, pimply skin and buck teeth. She was also the owner of the biggest breasts in San Francisco, and many a prospector had tried to stake a claim in the twin hills of her bosom. By and large they were unsuccessful, however, since Sarah Mindl (most of the time) was saving herself for someone better, a man of sensitivity and learning, a scholar who had more on his mind than her father's money or her own mammaries. She carefully poured the tea into each cup, pausing just slightly longer than necessary before Julius Rosensheine, one of the six Rosensheine sons who ranged in age from ten to twenty-five. Their eyes met and Sarah's wide skirt brushed Julius's ankle. True, Julius wasn't exactly a scholar, but he was a gentleman and extraordinarily handsome.

Samuel Bender's other daughter, the younger, prettier, small-breasted Rosalie, prodded Sarah unobtrusively in the waist. Sarah sometimes forgot herself in Julius's presence, which irritated their father no end. Sisters had to look out for each other, Rosalie knew. Sarah moved on to Mr. Bialik.

"We have," said Samuel Bender portentously, "this morning received good news."

There were murmurs from the assemblage.

Bender held up a letter. "Our appeal to Cracow did not go unanswered. I read you the response from the council of rabbis. 'Dear Mr. Bender: We have forwarded your request to the head rabbi of the town of Kolomyja, and he has this day advised us of the outcome. This is to inform you that soon, God willing, you will have a rabbi and a Torah of your own!' "

There was a cheer from everyone present except Julius and Sarah. Even Rosalie was caught up in the mood.

" 'In January'," continued Bender, " 'Rabbi Avram Mutz left Galicia to join you in the village of San Francisco. Avram thanks you for the picture of your lovely family. He is looking eagerly forward to meeting your daughter Sarah Mindl with an eye towards matrimony.' "

Sarah Mindl dropped her teacup, shattering it and spilling dark liquid over the hardwood floor. "Papa—"

48

Bender looked up sternly. "Not now, Sarah Mindl."

Sarah knelt and scooped up pieces of china as Rosalie came over with a napkin. Why, Sarah wondered, was her father so incapable of feeling, of understanding? This is America, she'd explained over and over, to no avail. Marriages here are not arranged. Just because yours was set up by your parents doesn't mean mine has to be. There are plenty of learned men in this country to choose from. Her father had listened passively on each occasion. His arguments were always the same, affectionate but patronizing, delivered with an air of finality. Children had not the sense to be left with so important a decision as choosing a lifelong partner. The young let their loins rule their heads. Their experiences and circle of acquaintances were limited. From antiquity onward it had been a father's responsibility to look after the matrimonial affairs of his daughters, and this Samuel fully intended to do. Besides, what Jewish girl in her right mind wouldn't leap at the chance to have as husband a *yeshiva bucher*, a lifelong student? Did not the Talmud itself say, 'If you must, sell everything and marry your daughter to a scholar'?

Sarah Mindl had been upset. She had cried. She had thought of running away. She sulked and spent much time in her room. And Samuel had worried. A little voice in the back of his head kept saying: She is too homely to attract a nice Jewish man. Even the big bust is not enough. She'll end up with a *shaygets*, a drinker, a barroom brawler. Recently, he and Sarah had seemed to compromise. The Rosenshiene boy appeared to show a little interest; Bender agreed to wait. All right, the Rosensheines were no intellectuals—in the old country Jacob, the father, had been a candle maker—but still, there was hope. However, when the Jewish community decided to request the services of a rabbinical scholar from Europe, the opportunity and temptation had been overwhelming. Bender could not resist. Julius Rosensheine was a *pisher* compared to such a person.

Sarah Mindl looked up pleadingly. "But you said . . . "

"Go to your room," ordered Bender.

Sarah buried her face in Rosalie's apron.

" 'The new rabbi,' " continued Bender, " 'will be arriving on the ship, The President Washington; there is even a chance he will complete his journey before Passover. Of course, the uncertainties of travel may add a small amount of time, but . . .' " Bender continued reading mechanically. In his own mind he was certain. Rabbis occupied a special place in God's scheme. There would be no delays.

• • •

It was, perhaps, the most unusual sight Darryll had ever seen. They were rolling through the gorgeous Pennsylvania countryside, about three miles west of Lancaster, his brother Matt riding ahead of the team, Darryll on the wagon's seat, and next to him, standing up, facing the rear, a man wearing a black, circular cap and a crazy entanglement of straps and boxes was chanting and moaning in a foreign language. It was almost enough to make Darryll wish that what was going to happen would not happen, just so he'd have time to see more and ask more questions about the bizarre ritual.

After five minutes passed, Avram turned around and sat down. Darryll bit into the apple he'd been holding.

"You through now?" he asked.

"Yes," said Avram, removing the phylacteries and placing them in a velvet bag.

"What are them things?" asked Darryll.

Avram smiled. "I know they must seem strange. They're called *tefillin*. Where I come from, Jews wear them during *shachris*, the morning prayers."

"What's the boxes for?"

"They contain tiny parchments with passages from the bible."

"No kiddin'? Inside them things?" Darryll shook his head. "How come you was standin' an' bendin' up an' down like that?"

"It's called *davening*," said Avram. "A custom. The main part of a prayer is called *shemona esray—esray* means eighteen, for eighteen separate benedictions—and is always said silently while standing."

"You remembered eighteen separate prayers? Man, I can't even recall three or four."

"Nineteen, actually," said Avram amused.

"But you said that word—what is it, ezree—"

"*Esray.*"

"Yeah. You said it meant eighteen."

"It does."

51

"So how come the prayer got nineteen parts?"

Avram raised his eyebrows. "Jews are noted for many things," he said. "Consistency is not one of them." He removed the cracked photo from his coat pocket and studied it carefully.

"One more thing . . . " said Darryll.

Avram looked up, saw a sheepish look on his companion's face. "Ask," he said. "Don't be ashamed. You're curious, ask. How else can you learn?" He felt self-conscious. Only a few months earlier the head rabbi had told him the same thing.

"How come," said Darryll, "you was facin' the back of the wagon? Is that part of the religion like, you gotta face the back of whatever you're in?"

Avram struggled to control himself. The last thing he wanted was to insult this man without whom he would never get to San Francisco. "No, no," he said. "It's simply that whenever you *daven*, you're supposed to face east—towards Israel. For us, Israel is the promised land."

"Somethin' like California, huh?" said Darryll.

Avram tilted his head slightly. "Something like that," he said.

"Care for an apple?" asked Darryll.

"Thank you."

Darryll passed Avram a large, red fruit, glancing over his shoulder as he did so. He studied briefly the Bender family portrait, Samuel and Mrs. Bender in the rear, Rosalie and Sarah Mindl flanking them, a six-year-old boy on Mrs. Bender's lap, and an older brother poking his head through from the rear.

"That your family?" he asked.

"No, no," said Avram. "Not mine."

Darryll squinted. "Girl on the left got tits like a cow."

Avram bit into the apple.

Abruptly, Darryll pulled back on the reins and halted the wagon. He pointed to a narrow opening on their right, overgrown with trees and winter foliage. "Shortcut," he said.

"Pardon?" said Avram, "I'm not familiar with that expression."

Matt had turned his horse into the leafy pathway.

"Loggin' trail," said Darryll. "See, me an' Matt used to be in that business. This one here is gonna get you to San Francisco four days earlier." He whipped the horses forward and the wagon lurched into the opening.

Behind a clump of trees, Jones, the man who'd sold the wagon back to the Diggs brothers, watched silently as it rumbled by. As soon as it was past, he edged his horse up to the rear tailgate, leaned forward to tie the reins to one of the slats, then lightly vaulted onto a cloth suitcase. Inside, under the canvas, he threaded his way through barrels of provisions until he got to the front. For a moment he peered through an opening in the curtains, then he reached out, grabbed the collar of Avram's coat and yanked him roughly backward into the wagon. Avram shouted in surprise, startling the team of horses and causing them to careen forward in terror.

"*Vuss . . . vuss iz duss?*" stammered Avram.

53

Jones locked a meaty arm under Avram's chin, dug his knee into the small of Avram's back. Outside, Darryll futilely pulled on the reins and shouted "Whoa!" while Matt raced in pursuit of the runaway team.

Avram desperately fought to recall the correct English words. "Please! Sir. Hey—ow, please! What are you doing?"

Jones quickly rifled Avram's pockets, removing all the cash. When he'd finished, he spun Avram around and buried a hairy-knuckled fist full force into his stomach. Avram doubled over as waves of pain and nausea pulsed upward through his body. Jones stretched Avram out on the floor and yanked off his shoes.

"This is where all you Hebes keep your dough, ain't it," he said, feeling along Avram's socks.

Avram said, "Nnnn."

Jones peeled off the socks. "Damn!" he said. "That's all you got."

"Please," said Avram.

Jones rolled him over and punched him in the face, his knuckles driving upward into Avram's chin. Small chunks of apple flew out of Avram's mouth. Jones dragged the unconscious body toward the back of the wagon, lifted it over the tailgate, and pushed it unceremoniously out. His horse neatly sidestepped as Avram hit the ground. Jones raced back to the front and pushed through the curtains next to Darryll. Matt had just about drawn even with the team. Jones took out the money and began to count.

● ● ●

It was twenty minutes before Avram awoke. There was a fierce pain in his abdomen and trickles of blood oozed from his forehead, nose, and mouth. His head throbbed with a dull ache. Slowly, he forced himself to stand. There was no sign of the wagon, or Jones, or the Diggs brothers. Even when his head began to clear, Avram could not accept what his intellect told him: They were criminals, all of them. Right from the beginning. The entire thing, the story about the mother, the selling of the wagon—it was a sham, a confidence scheme designed to fool gullible, naive immigrants like himself. He felt terribly angry, not so much at the beating he'd taken or at the robbery, but rather because he'd been so easily tricked, so childlike. He pictured them now, sitting somewhere, laughing at him. How had he been so effortlessly deceived?

He began to walk along the trail, feeling the rocks and fallen twigs cut into his feet. I am a simpleton, he thought, and God has seen fit to disgrace me because it is what I deserve. Shafts of sunlight filtered through the trees around him. Fleecy clouds scudded across a crystalline, cerulean sky. The air smelled of spruce and pine. Presently, Avram's step began to quicken. The pain in his stomach seemed to ease. His nature simply did not permit extended bitterness. The past was past; the future was too interesting to look backwards. It was the same characteristic that had made him a poor student.

After a while, he spotted a swath of color ahead on the trail. Coming closer, he saw it was one of his shirts. He picked it up and slung it over his shoulder. Three minutes later he spotted a shoe, then a sock, then another shoe. He put them on. Fifty yards farther along he found his Torah, half unfurled, lying by the side of the road. He lifted it, brushed and blew off the dust, kissed the parchment in profound, passionate gratitude. Thank you, Dear God, he thought, for sparing this most precious possession in all the world. Of course, the silver plate with the inscribed Ten Commandments was missing, but one miracle was enough. He staggered onward, cradling the Torah in his arms, glad of the extra weight, hugging it to his body. Soon after, he found a pair of his pants, then his *talis* and *telfillin*, his hat, and a bundle of papers. Farther down the path lay his *shofar*, his remaining sock, a pair of ice skates, a pile of underwear, and his prayer books. Finally, ten feet from the last item, lying on its side in a shallow ditch, he spotted his suitcase.

"This they couldn't throw out first?" he said aloud.

He stopped to rest. The trees on the sides of the trail had gradually thinned and he now found himself amidst gently rolling hills covered with low brush. Gingerly he probed the handkerchief he'd tied around his forehead; the bleeding had seemed to stop, although the dull pain persisted. He inhaled the clean, cool air. Could be worse, he thought. Could be worse. He continued on. A half hour later he passed a stone fence, looked out onto a furrowed field. Thirty yards away a group of men were plowing by hand. Avram threw his suitcase over the fence and scrambled after it. He squinted and began to make out details. Remarkably, the men were dressed all in black (he drew closer), had long, untrimmed beards (he was almost upon them), and black, broadbrimmed hats. Jews! thought Avram. Jews, here in America!

He broke into an awkward trot. "*Landsmen!*" he shouted. "*Landsmen!*"

The men stopped their plowing and looked up.

"Thank God, I've found you," said Avram in rapid Yiddish.

The men—there were three of them—stared without saying a word.

"A terrible thing happened," continued Avram. "I was going in a wagon to San Francisco. They beat me. They robbed me. . . ."

The tallest of the men shook his head.

"*Der koo toot meer vay,*" said Avram, pointing to the handkerchief on his forehead.

The tallest man turned to the farmer nearest him. "Is he speaking German?" he said in German.

The second farmer shrugged. "Maybe he has a speech defect."

Avram saw the blank looks, thought perhaps these Jews spoke only some local European dialect. "*Tsee ret daw ehmehtzer English?*" he asked.

"I think he's asking if we speak English," said the second farmer, still conversing in German. He took a step in Avram's direction. "Yes. Do you?"

Avram then saw an unbelievable thing. In the man's pocket was a Bible, the end protruding just enough so that a small cross was clearly visible. Avram's head began to spin. These Jews . . . were not Jewish! Christian Jews. Impossible. The man kept coming.

"*Oy gevalt,*" said Avram. He teetered for a moment, then passed out.

• • •

He awoke in a bed in a large room. Immediately, he looked around, saw his suitcase leaning against one wall. Two small boys, dressed in black clothing similar to that of the adults, sat in chairs near an oil lamp, watching him. As Avram's eyes opened, one of the boys called out, and a buxom, red-cheeked woman entered the room. She wore a long, dark dress, a gray bonnet, and a shawl.

"So, you are finally present," she said. "*We bisht?*"

Avram shook his head.

"It means, how are you?"

Avram squeezed his eyes shut, then opened them. "Where am I?"

"This is the Stoltzfus farm," said the woman. "I be Christina Stoltzfus and these be my sons."

Avram felt himself in a fog. "I—you're not Jewish," he blurted.

"Jewish? No."

"Are you Quakers?" He knew he was being grossly impolite, but he seemed unable to control himself.

"Quakers? No. Quakers say 'thee' and 'thou'. We do not," said the woman. "We are entirely different."

58

Avram heard a steady thumping on the single window, looked out and saw a driving rain.

"Yes," said Christina, observing him. "It makes down."

"It makes down," repeated Avram.

Christina studied him appraisingly. "Ain't you maybe feeling good?" she asked.

"Groggy," said Avram.

She shook her head.

"Sleepy."

"Ah, yes. Sleepy. Good. You sleep." She motioned to the boys. "Outen the light."

The older boy snuffed the oil lamp and within minutes Avram was again unconscious.

• • •

The next time he awakened it was dusk, and he was alone. He had not the slightest idea whether he'd slept one day or ten. He dressed himself quickly, feeling a bandage on his head when he put on his hat. He found his *tallis* in the suitcase, draped it over his shoulders, and quietly chanted *maariv*, the evening prayer. Twenty minutes later he pushed open the door and emerged into a spacious room where five people sat eating at a large wooden table.

"Ah!" exclaimed the man who'd approached Avram that first day in the field. "He comes! Our guest." Immediately, he rose and helped Avram to the table.

Avram recognized Christina and the two small boys who'd watched him while he slept. A third boy, in his teens, was introduced—"My son, Joshua"—and, finally, the farmer himself offered a gnarled hand: "And I am Daniel." Avram sat down.

"Take off your hat," advised one of the small boys.

"Shh!" said Daniel.

"No, no, he's right," said Avram. He removed his hat, placed it next to him on the floor. "I am Avram Mutz," he announced. "I come to America from Poland."

The boys began to titter. Avram saw they were staring at his skullcap, as were the adults who tried to mask their interest.

"A *yarmulka*," said Avram, pointing. "It *is* funny." He laughed also.

"You are Chewish," said Daniel. A half-question.

"Yes."

"We are Mennonites. You haf heard of us?"

"Just the name," said Avram.

"Here, they call us Amish," said Daniel. "There are other types of Mennonites who don't believe exactly as we do."

Avram nodded. "Jews, too, have differences," he said.

Daniel pointed to the table, as Christina thrust a plate in front of Avram. "Now, you eat," he said. "You are hungry?"

"Yes."

"Goot. Here iss to eat, I explain." The table was covered with the most enormous variety of foods Avram had ever seen, and Daniel ran through them all. "Fox grape jelly iss this one. Apple butter here. Ginger pears. Pickled beets over there, next to the pepper cabbage. In the big dish iss cabbage and boiled beef, to the right iss sauerkraut and pork, in the small platter iss green beans and ham. Dig yourself in."

"Well, I—"

"You know what you'll like"—Daniel patted his overhanging belly—"the *shnitz 'n gnepp*. There, in the corner. Joshua, pass it to Avram."

The boy handed a large plate to Avram, who gingerly set it down but made no move to touch the food.

"Nussing to be frightened," said Daniel. "Chust dried apples cooked viss dumplings in ham broth."

"I'm afraid," said Avram, "that—"

"You prefer maybe some cottage cheese?" He motioned to Christina. "Mama, bring some *shmeerkase* for our guest."

Christina disappeared into another room.

"You see," said Avram, "I am kosher. In the Jewish religion there are certain dietary laws. I . . ." He shook his head. How could he explain without insulting?

"You can't eat nussing?" asked Daniel.

"Only animals that chew their cuds and have a cloven hoof," explained Avram.

"Goot!" said Daniel. "Then the beef—"

"The cow must be killed in a special way. A rabbi must be there to inspect."

Christina returned to the dining room carrying a tray with several bowls. She placed them on the table.

"He can't have nussing," said Daniel. "Religion don't allow."

"Not even the pie?" asked Christina, looking hopefully at Avram. "It's called shoofly pie. It got molasses in it."

Avram sadly motioned no. Meat and dairy products had to be served and stored in separate containers. How could he be sure this was the case? "I'm awfully sorry," he said. "I mean no offense. Perhaps . . . there is some fruit outside?"

"At this time of year, nussing grows yet," said Daniel. "But maybe . . . last summer ve pickled some tomatoes. They are separate, in jars. This would be okay?"

Avram smiled. "Thank you," he said. "Yes. I think so." How could God resent one pickled tomato amidst all this splendor?

After dinner, Avram told what had happened to him on his journey—the voyage in steerage across the Atlantic, the missed ship in Philadelphia, the swindling and robbery by the Diggs brothers—and his need to make it, somehow, across the American continent. Daniel listened intently and sympathetically. Avram's best course of action, he suggested, was to catch a westbound train, which would be coming through in five more days. The station was not far from a farm owned by Daniel's brother; since Joshua drove his wagon there regularly anyway, he could take Avram without inconvenience.

"I . . . I am overwhelmed by your generosity," said Avram.

"Iss nussing," said Daniel, shrugging. "What else could ve do?"

For the next four days Avram lived on tomatoes, beets, apples, and fresh milk. Twice he went out with Daniel to help work the fields; the other days he remained with Christina and Joshua and assisted with various chores around the barn.

"You have a fine place here," Avram commented once, after they'd fed the horses. "Very beautiful."

Christina nodded and smiled.

"And a fine, big son," added Avram, nodding at Joshua.

"Soon, he be baptized," said Christina. "When he be eighteen."

"Very nice," said Avram. He glanced up at the barn. "You know, I've been meaning to ask you, is that a decoration?" He pointed to an elaborate, painted geometric design.

Christina looked up. "That? Oh no. That is very practical. Keeps the *hexa* from plaguing the livestock."

Avram knitted his brow.

"Witches," explained Christina.

Avram nodded. "Ah, yes. I see. Witches."

A few moments later, when Christina returned to the house, Joshua drew close and whispered, "Jewish people have no witches?"

Avram felt sheepish. "Well, we don't believe . . ."

"Myself neither," said Joshua. "Mama, I don't really think neither. Father, I think maybe."

"Well," said Avram, "it never hurts to be safe."

On the fifth morning, after a breakfast of apples and milk, Avram walked outside, suitcase in hand. Waiting for him, to his surprise, were not only the Stoltzfus family but also several men he'd worked with in the fields and at least five or six people he'd never seen.

"Good morning," said Avram to Daniel.

"Morning," said Daniel. "Nice day, say not?"

Avram nodded and moved toward Joshua, who was hitching a horse to a wagon. "I am truly sorry to be leaving," said Avram. "I wish, in some way, I could repay your hospitality."

"The boy goes again to his uncle in four days," said Daniel. "It wonders me that you would not wish to stay wiss us longer."

"I do wish," said Avram, "but there are people who wait for me in San Francisco. I thank you again."

Daniel helped Avram into the wagon while one of the other men stepped forward to hand up his suitcase. A very old man emerged from the small crowd.

"Ve haf decided you should haf ziss for ze train," he said, placing a small pile of bills in Avram's hand and forcibly closing Avram's fist around it. "Akron iss a far trip and only it sorrows us zat it can't be more. Ve say to you, *koom boll widder*, you understand?"

"I . . . think so," said Avram.

"Come again soon. Now you know." The old man stepped back.

"I'll write," said Avram, as Joshua climbed in beside him and the wagon began to move. He turned around and waved. "I'll never forget you," he called. "I promise. I'll write."

The countryside rolled swiftly by. It was a cold day, but not uncomfortable, and Avram was reminded of the weather in Galicia, of times spent outdoors when he was a child. "My grandparents used to have a farm," he said to Joshua.

"A farm like ours?" asked the boy.

"Oh not as big, not as good soil. But nice. I liked it."

"How is it you are not a farmer then?"

How to tell the boy about Poland's partition, the crazy Francis Joseph, the even crazier Nicholas, the shifting, kaleidoscopic laws and edicts that applied only to Jews? Impossible. "Well," said Avram, "God made me a rabbi."

"But why?"

"I guess," said Avram, "he had enough farmers."

The railroad station was a wooden shed with a ticket office at one end. Avram and Joshua watched as the train slowly pulled in, its boiler hissing and throwing off great geysers of steam.

"I'd like to go to San Francisco," said Joshua.

"Maybe you will someday," said Avram.

"No," said Joshua.

"But how can you be sure?"

"Because it is planned. Next year, after I am baptized, it is arranged for me to be married. Papa says I must have responsibility."

"I see."

Joshua leaned close. "If I tell you something, could you secretly keep it?"

"Who would I tell?" said Avram.

"I don't want responsibility. I don't want to be married."

"Well," said Avram, "it's understandable. It's not crazy."

"It's not?"

"I don't think so."

"I don't even want to be a farmer," said Joshua. "A sin, yes?"

Avram shook his head. He watched as several people boarded the train. "Not in my opinion."

Joshua looked around. "But it is a sin that I don't want to be Amish, eh?" He nodded. "*That* is surely a sin."

"That one, yes," said Avram, feigning gravity.

"Why?"

"Because you are what you are. To deny yourself is to dispute God for creating you as he did."

"Have you ever wanted not to be Jewish?" asked Joshua.

"No," said Avram quickly, looking away. Slowly, he turned back. "Once," he said. "When I was ten years old. Soldiers came to our village. They wore red uniforms with gold braids and metal helmets that gleamed in the sun. It seemed to me they were invincible. They had long swords and black horses. And that day I wished I wasn't Jewish so I could be one of them."

"Jewish men do not fight?"

"Sometimes yes, sometimes no. Sometimes only with Jewish women. The governments keep changing the rules about letting us in the army. At that time it was no."

"Amish men too," said Joshua. "You see these?" He indicated the hooks and eyes fastening his coat. "We are not permitted buttons. It reminds too much of the military."

66

"It's not such a terrible thing not to fight," said Avram.

Joshua stared at the ground. "When I go into town to buy things for my father, people laugh at me."

"Me, too," said Avram.

Joshua grinned. "They laugh at you because you look Amish."

"And they laugh at you because you look Jewish."

They both began to laugh at each other. Avram reached over and pulled down Joshua's hat until it was stopped by his ears. Joshua did the same to Avram. They were still giggling when the train whistle sounded.

Avram hugged Joshua tightly in his arms. "I'll miss you," he said. And then, pushing away, "Be true only to yourself, and God will be proud of you." He ran toward the train; he saw Joshua waving forlornly as he climbed aboard.

● ● ●

Avram sat near the window and watched the countryside hurtle past. The train was a fairly new one, with several modern conveniences. The three passenger cars were each equipped with stoves for heat, and a trainboy came around from time to time selling fruit and sweets. Although there were no sleeping facilities, the train did have a powerful whale-oil lamp to serve as a headlight for running at night. According to the man next to Avram, this was a considerable improvement over the older method of having the locomotive push a flat-car on which a pine-wood fire burned. Mr. Pennington, as he'd introduced himself, appeared to be quite experienced in railroad matters.

"In the business for twenty years," he told Avram. "Worked with Isaac Dripps himself when he built the John Bull back in 'thirty-one. Ever hear of the John Bull?"

"No I haven't," said Avram.

"Ran 'er up near Bordentown, New Jersey. First train with a cowcatcher." Pennington paused. "'Course, mostly it killed the cows instead of caught 'em, but that's the price of progress, isn't it?"

"I suppose so," said Avram. He glanced across the aisle at a woman sitting with three little girls. For a moment he was reminded of Sarah Mindl.

"Happen to notice the sand boxes on the back of the locomotive?"

Avram shook his head.

"Those were my idea." Pennington smiled at Avram, a florid face peeking out from between a bushy handlebar mustache and a bowler hat. "Can you guess what they're for?"

Avram wasn't terribly interested in mechanical things, but did not wish to be impolite. "To put out fires, I imagine," he said.

Pennington chuckled. "That's what most folks think, but it ain't so. Started back in 'thirty-six, actually. There was a plague of grasshoppers in Pennsylvania, kept gettin' on the tracks an' causin' all sorts of accidents. They tried everything to get rid of the little buggers: track walkers sweeping with brooms, scrapers on the cars, you-name-it. None of it worked. Finally, I come on this idea of puttin' sand boxes on the locomotives so's you'd have streams of sand hittin' the rails ahead of the wheels." Pennington snapped his fingers. "Worked like a goddamn charm," he said. "Like a charm."

Avram nodded stiffly.

"Oh, you're insulted now 'cause I used the Lord's name in vain," said Pennington. "Sorry if I offended you. Just kind of slipped out there." He laughed nervously. "Shows you the company I keep." There was a period of silence, and then Pennington said, "You, uh, Quaker or somethin'?"

"Amish," said Avram.

"Ah, Amish, uh huh. Yeah, I heard of that. I'm a Methodist myself."

"Very nice," said Avram. Outside, a stand of trees whizzed by so rapidly that individual branches were just a blur. "How fast do you suppose we're going?"

Pennington leaned forward. "Damned near sixty miles an hour, I'd say. Uh, I mean, uh, sixty."

Avram tugged at the window. "I wonder what it feels like," he said. "The breeze, I mean."

"Wouldn't try it if I were you," said Pennington.

"Why not?"

"Sparks from the smokestack. Fly all over the place. Burn the ass off you."

"I'll do it quickly," said Avram. He lifted the window about halfway, and stuck his head outside. The rush of air pounded against his cheeks. Impulsively, without thinking, he launched a gob of spit toward the front of the train, and a quarter second later received a faceful of his own saliva. Quickly, he retreated inside.

"Get hit by a spark?" said Pennington.

"I managed to douse it." Avram wiped himself off.

Across the aisle, the oldest of the three girls —Avram judged her to be no more than nine or ten—was leading her mother and little sisters in a game of Simon Says.

"Simple Simon says, 'Put your fingers on your nose.'"

The mother and middle sister obeyed, but the youngest merely tittered.

"Come on, now, Mary Beth," said the mother, "Jane said to put your fingers on your nose."

"You mean, Simple Simon said it," said Jane. "He also said, No laughing."

The little girl complied, and Avram smiled broadly at Jane, who regarded him sternly. Pennington got up and strolled to the end of the car, stretching his arms and legs as he did so.

"Simple Simon says, 'Put your fingers in your ears'," said Jane.

Avram stuck his thumbs in his ears.

The mother tapped Jane on the knee. "Don't bother the man, honey."

Jane slyly turned in Avram's direction. "Simple Simon says, 'You're not allowed to play.'"

Embarrassed, Avram lowered his hands and returned his attention to the passing scenery. He felt Pennington thump into the seat next to him and was about to ask how a train could be stopped in an emergency—and then he saw that it wasn't Pennington. A tall, buxom woman had taken Pennington's seat, had pushed over so close to Avram that they were almost touching. He glanced quickly at her and then looked away; she was smiling. Slowly, he let his gaze drift back. The woman was wearing a bonnet and long skirt, but it was her bodice that drew Avram's attention. Huge globes of white flesh bulged out and over. Avram swallowed and blushed; the woman continued to smile seductively. Sex posed a great problem for Avram. He greatly desired to have a woman and often found himself afflicted with lustful thoughts. Sometimes, at night in Kolomyja, legions of women had done command performances in his head, bending over so he could see their ankles and calves, carelessly revealing the reddened circle around a nipple, on one occasion even giving him a fevered glimpse of thigh. Women excited and tormented him. They were so different, all of them, so exotic: their silken voices, alluring perfumes, their slender hands, their breasts, their menstruations and special washings, their piled-up hair and fantastic underclothing. . . . God, the list was endless; it was enough to drive an honest man mad. The train lurched and swayed from side to side, and the woman allowed herself to bump against Avram repeatedly, brushing his shoulder with hers. Avram felt an ache in his loins, an insistent, unremitting pressure. It seemed to him he was about to burst. For a moment he thought of sticking his head out the window again, but decided instead to rise and stretch.

"Excuse me," he said, and pushed past the

woman into the center aisle. There was momentary, explosive leg contact, and then he was free, heading toward the lavatory at the rear of the car. Inside, a man stood staring at the mirror above a porcelain washbasin. His hat hung on a peg next to a towel.

"Excuse me," said Avram. "Are you finished here?"

"Be about a minute," said the man.

Avram stepped into the stall and closed the door. May as well use the time to good advantage, he thought.

The man at the mirror, Tommy Lillard, had much the same idea. He rinsed his face carefully with water, then patted himself dry with the towel. He viewed his reflection from several angles, smoothing down some errant hairs, sucking in his lips to make them somewhat thinner. Overall, he was quite pleased. His image would not be sullied. He removed the bandanna from around his neck, folded it so that it formed a perfect triangle, then meticulously tied it over his face. A minor adjustment was needed to make it ride higher on his nose. No need, after all, to have the bump show out. He narrowed his eyes as he reached for his hat. The tilt on his head had to be perfect. He fussed with it until he was satisfied. "Not bad," he whispered. "Not bad."

"Pardon?" said Avram from the stall.

"I said, 'Not bad'," said Tommy.

Avram shrugged. There was a rasping sound as Tommy drew a pistol from one of his two holsters. He spun the barrel to check that it was fully loaded, inspected the hammer, then quickly reholstered it. "Have a good day," he said as he left the compartment.

"Same to you," called Avram. "Go in good health."

Tommy stepped out into the center aisle and drew both his guns. "Ladies and gentlemen," he announced, "may I have your attention, please?"

(4)

Tommy Lillard was born on January 9, 1814, one day after his father died in the great battle against the British at New Orleans. "Died fer nothin'," Tommy's mother would say years later, and indeed it appeared so. Andrew Jackson had indisputably won a smashing victory—although it was learned after the battle that a peace treaty had already been signed. At the time of his birth Tommy had two older brothers and a sister, all of whom lived with his mother on a small farm outside Augusta, Georgia. Their principal crop was corn, which they consumed themselves, supplemented occasionally by two or three acres of cotton which they sold for cash. They had one slave, a fifty-year-old man named Jeb, who ate at their table, slept in the house and worked no harder in the field or around the barn than any member of the family. One day, when Tommy was eleven, Jeb announced at lunch, "Ah's goin' now," and shortly thereafter left the house and headed north on foot. The Lillards never saw him again and, since they'd never thought of him as "property," made no attempt to dissuade him or have him restrained. A year later, the corn crop was afflicted with an unknown disease and failed completely. The supplies of cornbread and grits were quickly consumed; the livestock that provided milk and meat could not be fed. The oldest of Tommy's brothers shipped out from Charlestown on a whaler. Two-thirds of the farmland was sold. Jonas, Tommy's middle brother, stayed to look after the remaining portion, while the rest of the family accompanied his mother to a nearby plantation where she worked as a domestic servant. The pay was good, a dollar a week (a Caucasian domestic was highly prestigious), and at least she could remain fairly close to home. Twice each month Tommy would return to visit Jonas, keep him company, hunt, and help out with the chores. When he was seventeen he took a job with the railroad, laying track along the Savannah River, his body drenched with sweat, muscles aching— and he began to wonder if manual labor would be his destiny in life. Then, in 1832, without warning Jonas simply abandoned the farm, joined the army, and was promptly killed at Stillman's Run in the Black Hawk war of that year.

His mother wanted Tommy to take over looking after the property.

"What for?" he asked. "Can't grow enough

corn to live on. Can't grow enough cotton to buy anythin' worthwhile. I say, sell whatever's left and be done with it."

"We're not sellin' unless we have to," said his mother.

"You have to," said Tommy.

He headed west. The examples of his father and brother had led him to a conclusion: If you were going to die, do it for yourself, not the army. Wars came and went; only the bigshots benefited. A man (he considered himself a man) had to actively control his own fate. Those who waited around, who depended on nature, on fortune, on benign neglect, sooner or later paid the price. In 1833, Tommy Lillard crossed the continental divide three months after his nineteenth birthday. He became a trapper, since it seemed to him the kind of occupation that offered the greatest independence, the least responsibility, and the chance to become rich. Starting from the Great Salt Lake, he followed the beaver south all the way to the Colorado River, took a Mojave squaw for a wife in 1834, abandoned her six months later somewhere in the San Joaquin Valley. At the Horse Creek rendezvous in 1836, loaded with pelts, he earned six hundred dollars, of which a hundred was used to purchase guns, knives, blankets and a new mule, two hundred to mail home to his mother and sister, fifty for whiskey, and the remainder gambled away. He headed north to the Columbia River, where in the winter of '38 a grizzly almost ripped off one of his ears, a friend managing to save it by using needle and thread to stitch it to his torn scalp.

Tommy was content these years, his own

man, answering only to his whims, moving when and where he pleased. Someday, in a vaguely imagined future, he saw himself settling down, perhaps with one of the Indian women who made such excellent bedmates and companions. Then came two bad seasons, in '41 and '42, and he knew the palmy days were numbered. Entire valleys that once rang with the sound of slapping beaver tails were now still. In large regions the animal had literally been trapped out of existence. In addition, the principal use for beaver pelts, the matted felt of men's tall hats, had been superseded by a new and explosively popular replacement—fine silk.

"Got to find us somethin' else," said Tommy's friend Jebediah Collins, the one who'd sewn back his ear.

"Like what?" said Tommy. "I give up farming, an' I'll be damned if I'm gonna scout for th' army like all them others."

"Wasn't thinkin' of farming," said Jeb. "Had more in mind the railroad business."

Tommy looked at him quizzically as Jeb smiled.

Three months later the two of them lay side by side near a curving, fifteen-mile-length of track in Fond du Lac, Wisconsin. Tommy was shivering uncontrollably as a slowly moving train came into view, steam hissing from the engine. At that moment he would've worked a year on a farm for nothing if somehow he could've abandoned his commitment.

"What you shakin' fer?" asked Jeb.

"Scared shee-it," said Tommy.

"That's good. Good for your body."

The train slowed even further as it hit the curve, and suddenly the two of them jumped on the running board. They pointed their guns at the engineer and fireman who immediately threw up their hands and begged them not to shoot. "Just tell us what to do," they pleaded.

"Git off," said Jeb, and the two trainmen leaped to the ground.

Tommy looked back at the passenger cars, saw one of the windows lift and a pistol poke out. A blast from his shotgun shattered the window's glass and the pistol was quickly withdrawn. The train rolled to a stop and the two men started back through the cars. The passengers were ordered to stand between the seats with their hands up. Salesmen and farmers, soldiers and businessmen—all complied when they saw Tommy's guns. Systematically, Jeb relieved each of them of their money and valuables.

"I'm gonna remain out here while my pardner goes through the next car," Tommy improvised as they left. "Anyone pokes his head out gits it blowed off."

They proceeded through the train until they came to the last car, a sleeper. A conductor blocked the door.

"You cannot go in there," he said. "There're women inside, and they've already been disturbed quite enough."

Jeb thrust his pistol up against the man's uniform so hard that one of the buttons actually wedged itself in the barrel. Jeb shot it out, and the conductor began to whimper. Tommy opened the sleeper's door and stepped into the car. A fat

79

man met him at the entrance. He was struggling to put on some outer clothing.

"Above all, no shooting," he said. "Don't be crazy."

"Sorry," said Tommy. "Too much excitement." He fired his shotgun through the roof, after which Jeb yelled for everyone to line up. A tall man in silk hat and pajamas forked over fifty-seven dollars. An old woman produced a diamond brooch. A blond-haired, distinguished looking lady began to laugh hysterically. Tommy walked down the aisle while Jeb stood cover. He collected everything, valuable or not. Watches, rings, purses, whiskey flasks, candies, wigs, even false teeth—all went into the suitcase he held open in front of him. An attractive woman, wrapped in a blanket, touched his hand as he picked up one of her stockings.

"Take me with you," she said.

"Why?"

The woman shook her head. "I don't know, it's, well . . . it's a very brave thing you're doing."

"Thank you," said Tommy, emptying several rings and bracelets from the stocking into the suitcase. "But it's just—"

"Also, I love the smell of gunpowder," she added quickly.

"Sorry," said Tommy. "Maybe some other time."

He gave the usual warning when he came to the end of the car, and then he and Jeb jumped off. Their horses were fifty yards away; two hours later they were counting their money.

"Over four hundred dollars," Tommy announced triumphantly. But more than that, more than any material gain, was a realization that had dawned on him halfway through: It had been the most exhilarating experience of his life.

The second robbery was easier, the third easier still. They learned to be efficient, to fire their guns as often as possible for the frightening effect, to avoid jewelry and other goods since they were too cumbersome to carry, were of indeterminate value, and took too long to dispose of. They robbed trains all over the country, not concentrating their attentions on any one area, counting on poor interstate police cooperation to give them an advantage. Once, when they were in Georgia, Tommy returned to visit his mother and sister.

"Died of cholera," the plantation owner told him. "Been at least three years now."

Tommy went back to business. It was so easy he could scarcely believe it. Most of the time the railroad owners were uncooperative with any detectives performing an investigation. Management was concerned lest the news of a robbery leak out and frighten away prospective passengers. Often, they even reimbursed people whose money had been stolen. Officially—as far as they were concerned—the crime did not exist. And then, in 1846, just outside of Abingdon, Virginia, a soldier—a passenger during a robbery in progress—made a sudden movement that startled Jeb Collins. Reflexively, Jeb pulled the trigger on his shotgun, leaving a bloody pulp in place of the soldier's head. Immediately, Tommy and Jeb jumped from the train. Women were screaming and crying hysterically.

"It's the end," Jeb said, a half hour later.

"Why?" said Tommy.

"They be comin' for us serious now."

Tommy nodded. Jeb, of course, was right. Eventually, everything ended. Good and bad. Farming and trapping. He thought back to the time he worked on the railroad that bordered the Savannah River. Build 'em one year, rob 'em the next. He wished things could stay the same.

"I'm headin' back west," Jeb said. "Maybe cut over down to Texas or Mexico. Once I get past the Mississippi I'm as good as gone. Ain't no one gonna find a mountain man when he don' wanna be foun'." He paused. "You comin'?"

Tommy shook his head. "Not me, no sir. Not yet."

Jeb shrugged. "One day, they gonna catch you."

"Maybe," said Tommy.

"So whyn't you quit?"

Tommy grinned. "I like it too much," he said. "A man just can't abandon his life's work."

"Up to you," said Jeb. He held out his hand, and Tommy shook it. "It really is over," he said.

"I suppose," said Tommy. "I suppose."

In September of 1849, Jeb Collins was shot dead in an argument with another prospector over a claim near Stockton, California. The claim later proved to be worthless. Tommy Lillard was still back east, robbing trains.

●　●　●

Avram was still in the lavatory.

"I want you all to be calm and listen to me," Tommy was saying to the people in the railroad

82

car, "because I'm only going to tell you this once." He waved his pistols.

"Please," said the conductor, "there's women and children here. Please, no shooting."

"Fine with me," said Tommy. "There's a man behind you with a big shotgun, but don't turn around."

The conductor stiffened. A woman began to moan.

Always the same, thought Tommy. Always the same. "Now this man don't care to be recognized," he said, "so I want everyone to take it nice and easy. Those who don't believe me are gonna die. . . ."

The mother of the three girls who'd been playing Simple Simon started to cry.

"Now," said Tommy, "I want everybody to put their hands on top of their heads."

All the passengers complied.

"Okay," said Tommy. "That's good. That's real good. Now let's play like we's all in church." He motioned to the conductor. "You, gimme!"

The conductor removed his hat.

"Now we goin' pass this around," said Tommy, "an' I want ever'body to be real charitable, hear?" He jammed the hat in the stomach of a fat man next to him.

"I don't have—"

"Fill it!" demanded Tommy. He cocked one of the pistols.

The fat man deposited a wad of bills.

Tommy stared at him coldly. "That's not yer whole poke, is it," he said flatly.

"It is," insisted the man. "It is. I—"

Tommy put one gun barrel up against the

man's cheek. "How'd you like a new nose-hole?" he asked. "You jes' tell me where you wan' it. Or maybe you'd like a new asshole instead?"

The man began to quiver, then reached inside his trousers and pulled out several more bills. They fluttered down into the conductor's hat.

"See what you can do if you try?" said Tommy. "That's as pretty as fresh snow." His voice hardened. "Now pass that hat around."

Quickly, the man handed the hat to a woman next to him.

"No buttons, rings or watches," said Tommy. "No objec's of sentimental value. Jes' cash, now, hear?"

The hat was moving briskly down the aisle, Tommy watching it carefully.

"An' you ladies," he added, "no tryin' a hide nothin' in your private parts." He saw a young woman look up. " 'Cause this ole boy got lots of experience in that sort of thing, an' if I suspects someone, I gonna have to give 'em a personal inspection, which they might not appreciate."

The young woman reached somewhere deep inside her clothing and came up with a large coin.

Tommy walked to the middle of the aisle and jabbed a sleeping farmer. He watched as the man came groggily awake. "Hey," he said, "no sleeping during the sermon."

"Whuh?" said the man, his voice sluggish, eyes still half closed. "Sorry, Father," he mumbled.

Tommy prodded him again, harder, and this time the man sat up. He was wearing torn

84

overalls and a bandanna similar to Tommy's.
"Your contribution?" said Tommy, holding out
the hat.

"Oh Jesus," said the farmer. "Hey mister,
please, come on, it's been a bad year . . ."

"Not fer me," said Tommy. "Now fork over!"

The farmer reached into a pocket and produced four bills and some change. Tommy
looked on disgustedly. He handed two of the
bills back. "Here," he said. "You need it more'n
I do."

By the time he got to the rear of the car the
hat was full. Tommy opened the door to the vestibule. He bowed. "I'd like to thank you all very
much fer your kind contributions to my cause."
He raised his voice in a pretense of speaking to
someone at the other end of the aisle. "Jake, I'll
be jumping here, you follow me at the next
bend." He looked around. "Remember, folks, if
you want to keep your heads, rest your hands on
top of them and don't turn around. Anyone
imagines they is a hero, mah advice is think on
it apiece. Who you helpin'? Whose money you
savin'? What's the chance you goin' be blowed
off the earth?" He nodded. "Afternoon, now."

A moment later he disappeared into the
vestibule, and a moment after that, as the train
slowed, he leaped down an embankment.

A second later, Avram emerged from the
lavatory. He hoped Pennington would be occu-
pying his seat next to the buxom woman, so that
he could find a place somewhere else. He'd had
enough temptation for one day. He walked down
the aisle, saw all the passengers with hands on

85

their heads. He smiled, and glanced at the three little girls. The buxom woman had shifted her location, and Avram slipped in next to Pennington, who also was playing the game. Avram waved at Jane, the oldest girl. Nice, he thought, that everyone was so friendly. He waited awhile, and then, when no one moved, he called loudly, "Okay, everybody laugh."

Nobody made a sound.

Avram chuckled. "Okay. Simple Simon says, 'Everybody laugh'."

Still, no one moved.

"I said, Simple Simon says." Avram now began to cackle uproariously. His shoulders shook. "Come on!" he yelled. "Come on!"

Not a single person so much as cracked a smile.

After three minutes, Pennington whispered from the side of his mouth, "Keep laughing, shmuck, and you'll be holding your head in your lap."

Avram, puzzled, could make no sense at all of the remark.

They made a water stop at a small station near a town called Summitville. Avram got off the train with his suitcase and stretched his legs. It was 6:15 P.M. He studied the sky, which was streaked with the mournful grays and scarlets of a fading day in early spring. He shook his head sadly, watching as a few people departed the station, met by carriages or small wagons. He began to walk along the side of the tracks, continuing in the direction the train had been

86

headed. Suddenly he heard the blast of the whistle, saw the great spouts of steam issue from the locomotive.

"Board!" came the conductor's voice.

Avram kept walking. Slowly, the train began to roll. As it passed him, he saw Pennington's face pressed against the window. He was gesturing to Avram, waving wildly, shouting something unintelligible. Avram waved back. "Don't open the window," he said quietly. "Sparks, you know."

The sky began to darken as he trudged along. The sun was a dusty crimson disk melting into the horizon. He came to a pond about thirty yards from the track. Two fishermen looked up as they saw him.

"Excuse me," said Avram. "You could tell me, please, how far away is Akron, Ohio?"

"I'd say 'bout forty-five miles," said one of the men. "Could be fifty."

"*Oy*," said Avram. "All right. Thank you." He resumed walking.

"Hey!" called out the man.

Avram stopped, turned. "Yes?"

"You just come off that train?"

"Yes, I did."

The fishermen glanced at each other. "There ain't no towns 'tween here an' Akron. You shoulda stayed on."

Avram shrugged. "I just feel like a little walk."

The men watched him suspiciously as he trudged along. How can I tell them, thought Avram, that a Jew cannot ride on a Saturday,

87

and that furthermore, for us, a Saturday begins on a Friday. How can I tell them?

Alone, in a field, Avram donned his *talis* in the fading light, removed two candles from his suitcase, and placed them in tiny holes in the sod. He lit the candles with a match, closed his eyes and drew his palms over the flames. "Blessed art Thou, O Lord our God," he intoned, "King of the Universe, Who has sanctified us by Thy commandments, and has commanded us to kindle the Sabbath light." In his mind, Avram created a picture: his mother placing two freshly baked *challas* at the head of the table and covering them with an embroidered cloth, his father reciting *Kiddush* and sipping wine from the nearby goblet. Occasionally, Avram knew, there were times when they couldn't afford the wine and had to borrow some meager droplets from equally poor neighbors. No matter. The sabbath was a special time, an occasion when even the lowliest, least consequential, most wretched individual could feel himself exalted, could feel himself miraculously blessed by the Almighty's special concern. Avram gazed up at the sky. In the east a crescent moon was visible; near it, the planet Venus was a diamond pinpoint of reflected light. Avram began to *daven.*

He spent the next day in the open, taking short walks but returning to the same spot. The *Shabbes*, after all, imposed certain limitations. You couldn't carry anything, tie a knot, write, ride, or work . . . and neither could your beast of burden, if you had one. The choice of remaining activities available was therefore not extensive.

Avram spent the day praying and reflecting on those portions of the *Mishna*, the codified Oral Law portion of the Talmud, that dealt with questions of ethics. It was as good a way as any of keeping his mind off his hunger. In late afternoon, he found some wild berries, which he ate ravenously, pretending they were bits of potato *kugel* and *gefilte* fish.

"Will you pass the horseradish?" he said to no one in particular.

Saturday night, he again slept in the open air, returning early Sunday morning to the train station.

"One-way to Akron, please," said Avram to the ticket agent. They were the only people at the station.

"Train ain't scheduled for five hours," said the clerk, peering through wire-rimmed spectacles.

"Fine," said Avram. "I can use the time."

"Plus, it never arrives on schedule anyway."

"Even better," said Avram.

The clerk regarded him curiously. "That'll be three-fifty," he said.

Avram reached into the suitcase, where he'd left his money. He fumbled a moment, then opened it completely. Gone! "My money!" he said. "It's not here!" He closed his eyes and began to sway. Such a shame, he thought. Because the money really belonged to the Amish people, and now their kindness would go for naught. Either he'd lost it somehow in transferring it from pocket to suitcase, or perhaps the two men he'd seen fishing had followed him and gone through his bag when he was asleep or away. (Actually, both hypotheses were incorrect. The money had been stolen by Mr. Pennington while Avram was in the lavatory.)

"I can't pay," said Avram forlornly.

The clerk withdrew the ticket.

"Is there any place here I can do some work?" asked Avram. "Anyone need some temporary help?"

The clerk narrowed his eyes. "Folks these parts mostly does their own chores." He shrugged. "Uh, what kind of work you lookin' for?"

"Someone, maybe, could use a rabbi?" said Avram hopefully.

"That's for Jewish folk, ain' it?" said the clerk.

"Yes."

"A Jewish priest."

"Well . . . similar."

The clerk nodded. "I seen a Jew once. Come to think of it, he had the long sideburns just like you. Left about two years ago, I recall."

"And there's no other Jews?"

The clerk wrinkled his nose. "I hear tell there may be a couple in Cincinnati."

"None here though?"

The clerk shook his head.

"Is there anyone else hiring?" said Avram. "For anything? Anything at all?"

"Nothin' I know of," said the clerk. "Unless you wanna work for the railroad. Got a gang layin' track about three miles from here."

"Show me the direction," said Avram.

The clerk pointed toward the east. "You just

follow the track and pretty soon you'll come to a spur. Follow it south and you can't miss it."

"Thank you," said Avram, hefting the suitcase. "I appreciate your recommendation."

"It's low-type business," said the clerk.

"Not as low as starving," called back Avram.

• • •

(5)

A long line of men stood before a table consisting of three planks placed across two sawhorses. Behind them, half-naked workers sweated and strained as they methodically laid a section of track. Sounds of steel hammers on steel rails reverberated off nearby trees. Avram waited, with his suitcase, just behind a Chinese man with a two-foot pigtail. Occasionally, the man would turn, smile sweetly, and then pivot back. After a while, he simply stared at Avram, then began to giggle uncontrollably—a soft, gurgling, Chinese-type chortle. Avram, delighted, laughed as well.

"Me Ping," the Chinese man said. "You funny looking fella."

Avram nodded. "Yes."

Ping nodded even faster, his smile covering

half his face. "You ever work on railroad before?"

"No," said Avram, eyes twinkling. "This will be my first time." He paused. "How about yourself?"

"Yes. Myself," said Ping, still grinning.

"I mean, is this your first time also?"

"Me? Oh, no. I work before. I show them. First, they say, China-man, he too small to work. Too skinny. I say, I work for you for free. You like, you pay. You no like, you no pay." He shrugged. "They pay."

"And you've been working since?"

"No since. What is 'since'? Work on track, bang with hammer."

"I see," said Avram, as the line slowly moved forward.

At the table, a redheaded man wearing a full beard, cap, and striped coat handed Avram a yellow card. "You get this stamped once in the mornin', once at night," he said. "Pay's by the week, twelve-fifty, plus all meals. You report to that tent"—he pointed to one of the two dozen tents set up—"and they'll assign you to a crew."

"Thank you," said Avram.

"Ever have any experience layin' track?" asked the man.

"I'm a rabbi," said Avram.

"Close enough," said the man, and waved Avram on.

The railroad camp consisted of tents to house the workers and supervisors, piles of wood that had to be made uniform in length to serve as ties, gravel for the road bed, wagons to haul supplies, horses to draw the wagons, a corral for the horses, and a pen for the cattle that provided fresh meat. All these features formed a sprawling, disordered agglomeration that oozed over the countryside at the rate of a mile a day.

"Remember," shouted the foreman of Avram's crew when they began work the next dawn, "a pound of tobacco to each man if we lay a mile and a half, and an extra day's pay if we make two miles. Now, let's hit it!"

The men began to work with a vengeance. There were a number of different tasks that had to be coordinated before actual track could be laid. First, the road had to be graded and a flattened bed made. Next, gravel had to be dumped so that the ties were held securely and did not move around. Then, after the ties were in place, the sections of rail had to be fixed to them with spikes. This latter job was the work assigned to Avram's crew—the sledgehammer gang. Stripped to the waist, except for his hat, Avram toiled alongside twenty other men.

"Eeeh!" said Mr. Ping as he hefted the hammer. There was a thudding, metallic clank when it struck the spike.

"Ihh!" said Mr. O'Leary next to him.

"Aye!" said Mr. Monterano, two men down.

"Oy!" said Avram, each swing of the hammer practically lifting him off his feet.

The sounds made a kind of harmonious progression.

"Eeeh!"
"Ihh!"
"Aye!"
"Oy!"
"Eeeh!"
"Ihh!"

"Aye!"

"Yow! Yaa!" Avram had staggered at the last swing, and his hammer had struck the ankle of a giant westerner next to him. Fortunately, the blow had not been full force.

"I'm terribly sorry," said Avram. "I beg your pardon. Please . . . excuse me."

Painfully, the westerner straightened up. "Yer excused," he said slowly. " 'Course, you do it again, I'm gonna have ta kill you. You unnerstan', I hope."

"Oh yes," said Avram. "Of course. Very reasonable."

Ping tapped him on the shoulder. "You, me, change places," he said. "Better for you."

Avram nodded, and they made the switch. "I appreciate it," he said.

"I have tlouble too when first start," said Ping. "I aflaid men call me Chink." He smiled. "But fear was baseless."

"I'm glad," said Avram.

"They call me slant-eye," said Ping, smiling. "Vely good name, I like vely much."

At night, after his evening prayers, Avram fell to the ground, exhausted. Every muscle in his body seemed to be screaming; even tiny movements were painful.

"It gets-a better, the longer you here," said Mr. Monterano, in the bedroll next to him.

"You'll be adjusted after about a year, me bucko," said Mr. O'Leary. "By then you'll be deaf, dumb, and blind, like the rest of us."

"Can't be any worse than the trip over," said Avram. "If I lived through that, *kinehora*, I'll live through this."

96

"Where'd you leave from on the other side?" asked O'Leary.

"Hamburg," said Avram. "And you?"

"Cork," said O'Leary. "We started with foive hundred people, ended up with two hundred less. Typhus, they said it was. Trip cost fifteen dollars. Imagine, payin' that much an' not makin' it. For that reason alone, I wouldn't give 'em the satisfaction of dyin'."

"I paid thirty-four," said Avram. "I wouldn't give them the satisfaction twice."

"We got thrown off our farm in County Kerry," said O'Leary bitterly. "Me, me brothers, me Mom an' me father. British bastards come an' kicked us right out when we couldn't pay the rent. Then a cousin of mine give us this booklet, *Hints to Emigrants from Europe*, by the Shamrock Friendly Association of New York City. It said that there were twelve thousand Irish in New York alone, and that pay for workers was good. That's when we decided to come over. Except the ship tried to land in Boston, an' they wouldn't let 'er dock when they heard about the fever. So we ended up in Canada, we did, an' we had to work our way back from there. 'Course there was only me an' me one brother by then; all the rest was gone."

"I'm sorry," said Avram.

O'Leary laughed hollowly. "Nah, don't be sorry. To lose everythin' just when paradise is within reach—that's what it means to be an Irishman."

Avram nodded. "And a Jew, as well."

"And an Italian," added Mr. Monterano.

97

The men waited, but heard nothing from Ping.

"How 'bout you, slant eye?" asked O'Leary.

Ping giggled softly. "Not me," he said finally. "What you think, everyone so foolish as you?"

* * *

By the end of the first week, unlike most of the men who gambled or bought liquor or sent money home, Avram still had his entire ten dollars and forty-two cents. (He'd taken off the Sabbath—the foreman had given him no problems—and thus was paid for only five days, since no work was done on Sunday.) On Sunday evening, he'd walked five miles to where a wagon train had camped and attempted, unsuccessfully, to purchase one of the wagons.

"I couldn't meet their price," he told O'Leary and Ping later, back at the tent.

"What was their price?" asked O'Leary.

"The wagon master wanted me to become a saint," said Avram. "I told him Jews don't have saints and if they did, I still couldn't be one because I would never be good enough."

O'Leary chuckled. "He meant Saint, with a capital S," he said. "That's how they call themselves. Everyone else calls 'em Mormons, an' hates their guts."

"Anyway," said Avram, "he told me no one had room for me, and that ten dollars and forty-two cents couldn't buy a wagon."

"Still don't understand why you wanna go," said O'Leary. "You get your three squares here, plus a decent wage, good companionship, work in the fresh air. . . ." He shrugged.

"He not dumb," said Ping. "You smart, you listen. We open big lestaulant. You work one year, have enough money to buy wagon. Maybe we go with you . . . open big joint, San Flancisco, sell Jew food, Chinee food, evelything. Even have take-out order."

"Please," said Avram softly, "show me where to buy a horse."

Monterano, who'd been listening, sauntered over. "Eh, Mr. Cauliflower, how you-a gonna know the way, huh? You getta lost, you gonna ride inna circles."

"Please," said Avram, "just show me where to buy a horse."

Ping shook his head and pointed to a tent near the corral. "There, maybe you can buy. But Monterano light. You clazy Jew boy. You gonna get lost."

Avram picked up his suitcase. "Believe me," he said, "I'm not clazy."

• • •

Avram was a mass of saddle sores. It seemed to him he'd been riding for months instead of ten days. A chill rain soaked his clothing through to his skin. He was immensely grateful when the pilot of the wagon train he'd been following sounded the noon trumpet and the wagons began to circle in the usual formation. Time and again Avram had been impressed by the precision with which over sixty vehicles could so quickly form a hundred-yard-diameter enclosure, the tongue of one chained to the tailgate of the next. He dismounted and watched as the herders drove the stray cattle and horses toward the new encampment. Within minutes, crude shelters had been erected in the circle, and smoke was visible from a half dozen fires. Avram walked his horse to a small tree and took what refuge he could under the leafless branches. He did not bother to tie the animal, as it had clearly established that it would not run off. Since he'd needed money to buy provisions, Avram had allotted only five dollars for transportation, and the result was a stringy, mangy horse with soft, downcast eyes, matted fur and a slight limp. Avram had decided to call him *Nuchshlepper*—a dragger, a straggler. It was clear to him from the first, of course, that the horse was Jewish.

Avram unpacked his bedroll and lay down under the tree, as Nuchshlepper grazed on some brownish grass. From people whom he'd passed, Avram had learned that they were following a trail called the National Pike, an extension of the old Cumberland Road. He was in Indiana now, heading west and south toward Illinois. Within twenty seconds, he fell asleep.

He dreamed.

It was Chanukah and he was a small boy. He was playing *draydl* with his friend Levi, and they were betting chestnuts on the outcome. Avram was behind by six nuts and was becoming testy. He spun the *draydl* fiercely and awaited the result. Levi got to it first. "*Shin*," said his friend exultantly. "You lose."

"Damn!" said Avram, and then, "You cheated! You didn't win. You're a cheat!"

Immediately, his mother appeared in the doorway. "I heard that, Avram," she said. "And it's not the first time today either. There's no excuse for that kind of behavior and you're going to be punished." She turned to Levi. "Levi, I'm afraid you'll have to go home. Avram is being punished."

Avram stood up, enraged. "It's not fair!" he shouted. "He's a damn cheat, he turned the *draydl*—"

"That's it!" yelled his mother, topping him in volume. "No potato *latkes* today, and no Chanukah *gelt*. Bad boys get nothing."

She turned and walked from the room.

Avram began to sob. More than the token gift of money—*gelt*—the potato pancakes were his favorite food in the whole world. He lived for those times his mother cooked *latkes* and now, to be deprived. . . . The tears cascaded from his eyes and down his cheeks . . .

Avram snapped awake. He sat up and wiped the wetness from his face. Though the rain had stopped, a branch overhead was dripping directly on him. He crawled to his feet. *Time?* he thought. How long?

He looked around frantically, saw Nuchshlepper grazing nearby in a vast, empty expanse of field. He ran to the top of a small rise and peered out across the prairie. Nothing. In the distance was the horizon. It took some time for the fact to register on his mind: *There was nothing there.* He searched the ground for tracks, but the rain had left only a muddy mess. Avram walked slowly back to his horse.

"So," he said quietly. "We're a little lost."

Nuchshlepper showed his teeth.

"This is nothing to laugh at," said Avram. "What, you think this is funny?"

Nuchshlepper shook his head.

"Don't worry, we'll keep going. The sun rises in the east and sets in the west, that much I know. We'll ride into the sunset, okay?"

Nuchshlepper, lost in thoughts of his own, didn't answer.

Two days later, outside Vandalia, a family of raccoons crept into Avram's camp near the banks of the Kaskaskia River. While he slept, while the early morning hoarfrost surrounded his body in a deathlike cloak, the raccoons broke into his waning stock of provisions and gorged on flour, beans, coffee, potatoes, chocolate, salt, sugar, and rice. An hour later, Avram woke. He sat up sleepily, then began to moan as he caught sight of the widely scattered remaining food and watched the last raccoon scurry away.

"You couldn't say something?" he shouted at Nuchshlepper in Yiddish. "You couldn't tell me, giving me a poke? A *shmendrick*, you are! A real *shmegegge!*"

The horse hung his head.

Avram pored over the ground, recovering a meager portion of the beans, some coffee, and a small tin containing garlic, pepper and paprika that the raccoons had either not wanted or hadn't been able to open. He rolled up his bedding and prepared to ride. He swung himself over Nuchshlepper's back and gently pulled upward on the reins. "All right," he said. "Don't sulk. It's not the worst thing. Next time you'll know better. Meanwhile, I've still got a dollar

thirty in my pocket, so we'll see what happens."
He squeezed the horse's sides with his knees.
"Come on, all's forgiven. We Jews have to stick
together, eh? Who else will look out for us?"

He taught Nuchshlepper to *daven*. At least
it seemed like *davening*. Wearing his *yarmulka*
and *talis*, Avram could get the horse to sort of
sway forward and back, pretty much in time with
his chanting. Once, he was tempted to put his
yarmulka on the animal's ears, but decided this
would be a profanation.

"You're a good man," he told the horse on
several occasions. "You don't whine, you don't
complain. A *shayner Yid*."

On the first day of May in the year 1850,
Avram crossed the Mississippi on a Mackinaw
boat, having booked passage for himself and
Nuchshlepper at Dube's ferry, some miles north
of St. Louis. The fare was seventy-five cents (a
special for immigrants; the price for anyone else
was a quarter). At a small outpost on the western
bank Avram used the remainder of his cash to
purchase some dried corn cakes, a few tins of
beans, and half a bale of hay for his horse. Four
days later, the food was gone.

Late that afternooon Avram saw a movement in the limitless expanse of prairie grass. He
reined Nuchshlepper to a halt, dismounted, and
peered myopically ahead. A flash of reddish
brown blended almost perfectly with the sur-
roundings. Avram fell to his knees and crept
forward. The prairie chicken had stopped and
was staring at something in its brainless, bird-

like manner. It cocked its head when it saw Avram.

"Hello, little *faygeleh*," he said sweetly. He clicked his tongue and the bird took two steps backward. "Here, little chickie. Here." The grouse retreated some more. "Come on, darling, Avram won't hurt you."

This was a definite lie, and the bird began to run.

"Chick, chick, chick, chickie, chickie!" said Avram. He rose and began to trot. The grouse stopped. Avram made several crude chirping and peeping sounds.

The grouse looked at him with disdain and began to run full tilt, Avram following.

"Wait!" he screamed. "Wait . . . hey, wait . . . wait!"

The bird opened a ten-yard lead and Avram gave up. He was winded and nearly exhausted. "You should *geh in dred!*" he shouted impotently, waving his fist. "*Geh kacken offen yom!*"

The prairie chicken disappeared in the grass. Avram walked back to his horse. "Up close, he didn't look tender," he explained, "so I let him go."

Nuchshlepper whinnied.

At dusk, Avram stood hip deep in a tiny tributary of the Osage River, trying to spear with a sharpened twig the fish that swam around him. He plunged his weapon thirty or forty times into the water, and came up with nothing. Nuchshlepper stood on the bank, drinking. Avram took aim at a particularly fat, luscious trout that had been lounging around his waist. He followed it, timed its movements carefully—and struck. Effortlessly, the fish dodged the thrust. Avram flung the twig in frustration . . . and suddenly the water in front of him exploded with a deafening roar. The trout that had teased him left a thick wake of blood as it floated to the surface on its side.

A miracle, thought Avram at first. In my need, God has performed for me a miracle. (Later in his travels he would continually reassess and evaluate that first reaction.) A second explosion followed, then a third and fourth and fifth. Avram's body was ringed with spouts of water; the river around him turned red with blood. A belt of maimed fish encircled his body. Fearfully, he turned around.

Tommy Lillard was standing with a pair of smoking Colt pistols, a large-gauge shotgun tucked under one arm. He wore black pants and a black leather jacket and watched Avram curiously.

"How hungry are you?" he asked.

"Well," said Avram softly, "I wouldn't have to force myself to eat."

Tommy fired one more time.

Avram glanced down as a new fish surfaced above his right thigh. When he looked back, Tommy had holstered his gun. "If you'd been here a little earlier," said Avram, "we could have had roast chicken."

• • •

Impaled on a twig, the last fish roasted above the small fire. Avram and Tommy sat on the ground nearby, finishing the remains of the five trout Avram had cooked earlier, spiced with paprika and garlic. Tommy licked each of his fingers.

"So that's Jewish cookin', huh?"

"Well," said Avram, hesitating, "*gefilte* fish and *kishka* it's not, but you get some idea, maybe."

"Never heerd of no filter-fish," said Tommy. "They fresh water or salt?"

"It's chopped up," said Avram. "Actually, it has several kinds of fish."

Tommy lit a cigar. "Where you comin' from?" he asked. "I know you ain't from aroun' here."

Avram nodded. "This is true." He pointed vaguely west. (Without the sun he was lost.) "Back there," he said.

"You from California?" asked Tommy.

"California is that way?"

Tommy stared at him. "You *lost*, ain't you?" He shook his head in wonder. When he'd seen Avram in the stream, stabbing at trout, he'd almost died laughing. He'd witnessed many things in his time, but this black-hatted, curly sideburned little man, hip deep in water, trying to spear a fish, had been among the strangest. "You *lost?*" he repeated again when Avram failed to answer.

"A little."

"A little," echoed Tommy. "You got any money?"

"No."

"Food?"

"No."

"Mmm." Tommy puffed on his cigar. "You sure talk funny. Where were you born?"

"Galicia," said Avram. "It's a part of partitioned Poland."

Tommy wrinkled his eyebrows. "That near Pittsburgh?"

"No, it's near Bohemia."

"Oh, yeah," said Tommy, feigning recognition. "Yeah, I heard a that one."

"And you?" said Avram.

"You wanna know where I'm from?"

"Yes. If you don't mind telling."

"I don' mind. I come up on a farm in Georgia. You know Georgia?"

"No," said Avram. "Sorry."

More honest than me, thought Tommy. "An' you're goin' to California, right?" he asked.

"Yes."

Tommy flicked off an ash. "You ain't gonna make it," he said flatly.

Avram shrugged. "Excuse me," he said, "but in the morning, you'll be kind enough to point out in which direction is San Francisco?"

"Sure."

"Thank you. Would you like to fight for the last fish?"

"Sure," said Tommy affably.

"Your choice of weapons," joked Avram.

"You think you got a chance?"

"I think I can say with confidence," said Avram, "none whatsoever."

Tommy narrowed his eyes. "You still hungry?"

"Yes."

"Help yourself."

Avram reached for the last fish. "You're a nice fellow," he said.

"I think you got a minority opinion," said Tommy.

"And why not? I'm a member of a minority."

Tommy ditched the cigar. "You got family waitin' on you?"

"Well . . . not exactly," said Avram.

"Hey," said Tommy, "that's a yes or a no. Either someone's your relative or they ain't. How come you always hedge?"

"I'm promised a wife when I arrive in San Francisco," said Avram, "but I've never met her."

Tommy shook his head in wonder. "You gonna marry someone you never seen?"

"Oh, I've seen her," said Avram. He reached into his pocket.

"I been married six times," said Tommy. "Only the women was Injun, so it don't count." He closed his eyes. "What qualities you think is most important in a female?" he asked, framing the words carefully.

"Well," said Avram, "myself, I would look for a religious spirit and appreciation of God, cleanliness and personal hygiene, a good cook, a laundress, someone who can raise children according to the law." He paused. "And you?"

"I look fer big tits," said Tommy. "Bigger the better. That's the trouble with them squaw-women, they got nothin' up top."

Avram produced the photograph of the Bender family. "They sent me this picture before I left."

Tommy studied the faded rectangle, his

108

eyes stopping and locking on Sarah Mindl. "Who-eee!"

"You're enjoying the picture?"

"I am indeed!" chortled Tommy. "Now that's my kind of woman." He looked up at Avram. "A good cook, eh? A laundress?" He poked Avram in the shoulder. "You son of a gun."

Avram smiled.

"You son of a gun, you," repeated Tommy. "*Shee-it!* Those things look like cannon balls under there. You're some sly operator! Gotta hand it to you."

Avram held out his hand for the photo.

"No, not this. This I wanna look at some more." Tommy shook his head. "Yes, sir. Yessireee. The other one ain't bad either, but the blonde is my meat."

"The other one is her sister," offered Avram.

"A l'il too skinny," said Tommy. "Nice face, but a l'il too skinny."After another moment he handed the picture back to Avram.

"You, uh, have any family?" said Avram.

"Used to."

"You don't see them any more?"

"Nope. Died. All of 'em except one brother who went off whalin' somewheres. Ain't seen him in years."

"Sorry," said Avram.

"No need ta be," said Tommy. "That's the way life is. The strong survive, the weak get eaten up."

"Perhaps so," said Avram, "although sometimes it's not obvious who is strong and who is weak."

Tommy grinned. "I'll agree with you there, friend. I'll agree with you there."

An hour later, they prepared for sleep. Avram removed his hat and laid it alongside his bedroll.

"How come," said Tommy, staring at Avram's *yarmulka*, "you wear one hat under the other? Seems a mite overcautious to me. I mean it's May, the weather ain't *that* cold. Besides, the inside hat don't look very warm to me."

"It's a religious tradition," said Avram. "Covering the head is a sign of respect before God."

"I thought *un*covering the head was s'posed to be respec'ful," said Tommy. " 'Course I ain't seen the inside of a church since I was ten, so a lot I know."

Avram stretched out his legs.

"What do you call the thing you are?" asked Tommy.

"Jewish," said Avram.

"No, no, I mean, like a reverend."

"*Rebbe*," said Avram, "or rabbi."

Tommy stared into the distance. "Well, rabbi, you ain't seen nothin' yet. . . . This country got mountain lions bigger than a horse. Snakes as thick an' long as full grown maple trees. They spit poison—kill a man at thirty yards."

"Is that right?" said Avram. "I wonder what such a creature would do to one of our Jewish *golems*."

"Golems?"

"They're beings that look like men, but have no souls. They walk around, but they're lifeless."

Tommy shook his head. "Yeah, I know guys like that."

110

"You have them here, too?" said Avram.

"Sure," said Tommy. "Most of 'em work in banks." He pulled off his boots and lay on his back. "But I'll tell ya, the things that are really scary are the bugs we got here. Some of 'em is so big they bite a man and drink all his blood in less than a minute."

"We got much worse than that in Galicia," said Avram.

"You do?"

"Sure. We have Cossacks. You know from them also, maybe?"

"Nope."

"They only come when it's dark. Midnight. And they never make a sound. Half of them is a goat and the other half is a man. They live deep in the forest, and the really big ones can fly."

"Fly, huh?" said Tommy. "No shee-it. What do they do to ya, these Co-sacks?"

"No one knows," said Avram. "To look at one is to die."

Tommy chuckled. "You ever heard of the three-headed, side-hilled wowser?"

"Oh, sure," said Avram. "We walk them on leashes."

"You do?"

"Well, only the blue ones, of course."

Tommy turned to him and grinned.

"The thing that frightens me," said Avram, "is a *dybbuk*."

"That's somethin' like a moose, ain't it?" said Tommy.

"I think you have it confused," said Avram. "A *dybbuk* is an evil spirit, a demon who takes possession of someone. The only way to get it

111

out is for a holy man to read the ninety-first psalm and then to blow a *shofar*—a ram's horn—next to the occupied body."

"That one give me the creeps," said Tommy, pulling his blanket over his shoulders.

"They say," said Avram softly, "that when a *dybbuk* leaves you, a bloody spot comes out on the little toe of your right foot. That's how you can tell if you've been possessed."

Slowly, Tommy's hand crept down his calf, then over his heel, and finally probed his little toe. Feeling no sore, he quickly withdrew it. He sat up and looked over at Avram. "Dang! You win. You lie better'n me, an' I lie with the best of 'em."

Avram yawned. "Who was lying?" he said.

Tommy lay down again and clicked his tongue. "Night," he said.

"Good night," said Avram. He lay awake for several moments, then pulled out the photograph he'd shown Tommy. He looked at Sarah Mindl, but found his eyes trying to drift, pulling away as if they had a mind of their own. Finally, tired, he let them go where they wanted and there, in the open prairie by the soft light of a half moon, they focussed in on the image that had compelled him from the first—the face of Sarah's sister, Rosalie.

• • •

The sun had just come over the horizon when Avram and Tommy finished saddling their horses.

"Nice meetin' up with ya," said Tommy.

"Nice meetin' up with ya," echoed Avram.

"You got them directions all figured out now?"

"Yeh, yeh, I got," said Avram. "Right from that tree I head straight north two or three days till I reach the flats. Then I turn left, which is west and go until I come to Independence. Right so far?"

Tommy nodded.

"From Independence, I go to Topeka, and then north and west along with Little Blue River until I get to Fort Kearny. From there, if I want to be killed by Cheyenne Indians, I follow the South Platte River. If I want to be killed by Arapaho, I follow the North Platte. Either way, I get back up to the Oregon trail until I get to Fort Bridger. From there I go up through the Rockies to Fort Hall, then continue—"

"Straight as piss—"

"Straight as piss across the Utah desert on the California trail."

"How'll you know you're goin' right?"

"I'll see, uh, the . . . mmm . . . Humboldt River on my left. I follow that till I come to Virginia City, then head through Kit Carson pass until Hangtown. From there I continue west till Sutter's Fort, keep going, keep going, then take a left, making sure the ocean's on my right shoulder, and just hot-tail it into San Francisco."

Slowly, Tommy shook his head.

"I made a mistake?" said Avram.

"Nope. No mistakes."

113

"It was good then?"

Tommy looked at him thoughtfully. "Real good."

"Then why . . . ?"

"I ain't never seen anyone with a better head for memorizin' directions, nor with a worse body for follerin' 'em."

Avram shrugged. "Could be. But, as they say, 'Az Got vil, shist a bezim oykh.'"

"Who says that?" asked Tommy.

"It's a proverb in my country," said Avram. "It means, 'If God so wills it, even a broom can shoot.'"

"Never seen nothin' like that," said Tommy. He reached out and shook Avram's hand. "Ain't no easy thing you're tryin', ya know."

"This I understand," said Avram.

"Lotta folks git starved on the way, their animals die, they freeze, they git killed by Indians, they catch fever. One year I seen maybe two hundred graves just on the California trail alone."

"Well," said Avram, mounting his horse. "I have one consolation. If I die of hunger I can't freeze or be killed by Indians."

"True enough," said Tommy, mounting his own horse. "By the way, you speak Spanish?"

"No. Why do you ask?"

"Case you end up in Mexico," said Tommy.

Avram nodded. "If you should come to San Francisco, I hope that you call on me and then we can talk over old times." He waved a final time, squeezed Nuchshlepper's sides, and they started off.

"Hey!" called Tommy.

Avram looked back.

"That way!" Tommy pointed opposite to the direction Avram had been heading.

"Of course, it's that way," said Avram, trying to cover his embarrassment. "I know it's that way. But first, I have to go around"—he glanced in front of him, saw a fallen tree—"that big log."

Tommy wrinkled his forehead.

"It's a custom," said Avram. "You conquer a small obstacle before you tackle a larger one."

Forgive me for lying, God, he intoned silently, but how can I let this wonderful man think me a complete fool? He guided Nuchshlepper around the tree, reappeared, and passed close to Tommy without saying a word. An instant later his saddle slid off Nuchshlepper's back, depositing him violently on the ground.

Avram got to his feet immediately, not allowing himself to rub where it hurt. "The buckle," he muttered. "I think it's defective." He shouldered the saddle for the second time that morning and laid it on his horse's back. He cinched the buckle carefully and remounted.

Tommy, who'd been watching incredulously, pointed to the rear end of his horse. "What do they call this in Jewish?" he asked.

"A *tuchis*," said Avram.

"Well, you keep your eyes on this too-cass," said Tommy, "an' don't take 'em off till you start to see mountains." He trotted off.

Avram, stunned, thanked God for this marvelous new good fortune.

• • •

(6)

West of Fort Kearny, Tommy and Avram
made their way down some steep hills. Below
lay the Platte River, winding its way through a
verdant forest redolent with the piquant, minty
odors of early spring. Suddenly, Tommy's horse
stumbled, tottered momentarily, then regained
its balance.

"Shee-it!" he said. "Don't get too close to
that edge."

Avram shortened Nuchshlepper's reins.
"What kind of a word is that?"

"Which?"

"You always, at certain moments, say, 'shee-
it'."

For an instant, Tommy was confused. "Shee-

117

it? *She*-it? Oh . . . sheeit. Oh, yeah, well. Ain't you got nothin' like that in your language?"

"Well, I don't think so. I—"

"What do you say when you're taken by surprise? When somethin' happens you wasn't expectin'?"

Avram considered. "Well, I guess, *Oy veh iz mir.* Or maybe, *Oy gevalt.*"

"*Oy veh iz mir,*" said Tommy. "I like that one. That's it. That's what 'shee-it' means."

Avram smiled and nodded. "Ah," he said. "That makes sense." Proof, he thought, that any two people, however disparate their backgrounds or characters, can, if they get to know each other, learn to communicate effectively.

• • •

Avram crept stealthily (he thought) through the tall grass. Abruptly, he stood up and began to run, swinging the tails of his long black coat and yelling, "Hey! Come! Let's go, you! Whoopee! Hey! Chickens! Come out!"

Ahead of him two grouse flew up from where they had taken cover. As they rose through the air, Tommy stood up from where he was concealed, raised his shotgun and fired twice. Both birds fell to the ground.

Avram retrieved the grouse and held them up as he walked forward. He was breathing heavily from his run. "So," he said, "tonight you feast."

"*We* feast," said Tommy. "Plenty there for us both."

Avram smiled sadly. "I'm tempted . . ." he said. "Believe me."

"You mean you ain't gonna have none?" said Tommy.

"Regretfully," said Avram, "no."

Tommy looked puzzled. "But I thought you said that there *kosher* business allowed as ducks and pheasants and quail was okay. That th' only birds you couldn't eat was eagles an' vultures an' owls an' things like that."

"The rules are complicated," said Avram. "Even I don't know all of them. But I do know the animal is not considered clean unless it's slaughtered in a certain way according to ritual. Its organs can't be perforated and it can't have any broken or fractured bones."

"Well, you tell me how the hell you goin' to catch you a grouse without fillin' it fulla buckshot."

"I can't," said Avram. "I tried once, but . . ." He shrugged.

"Danged if I know how you live," said Tommy. He took the two grouse that Avram offered. "You don' eat prairie chicken, you don' eat sowbelly, an' you don' eat rabbit. One day you jus' gonna bust open an' out gonna come a whole mountain a beans an' taters."

"I think," said Avram, "by this time they're digested."

They camped that night near a small stream, and kept their camp fire carefully shielded by a blanket draped over the low-hanging limbs of an evergreen. On the opposite bank, two hundred yards away, they could see, silhouetted in the moonlight, the conical tops of several dozen teepees.

"Pawnee village," Tommy had said softly.

Avram could distinguish several shapes moving at the outskirts of the grouping of wigwams. "Are they dangerous?" he asked.

"Hard to say," said Tommy. "They help the army, I know that. Scout for 'em an' all. But you never know. Lotta cholera amongst 'em, I heerd. Caught it from the white man. They do a lotta fightin' with the Dakotas but I suppose now, with the disease, they're mostly losin'."

Avram focused on a brave wearing only breechcloth and moccasins. The hair on his head had been shaved everywhere except for a narrow ridge from the forehead to the scalp-lock.

Tommy grinned. "That's the way they like it trained," he commented. "So's it looks like a horn. Crazy, huh?"

Avram ran his hands along his *peyess*. "Maybe, to them, we look crazy."

"They make it stiff with paint an' bear fat," said Tommy. "Stinks somethin' fierce in the summer."

Avram turned away from the village to face Tommy. "You know," he said admiringly, "you're a very learned man."

"Aw, I don't know much," said Tommy. "I just got a faculty for rememberin' what I seed."

"You know," said Avram, "in the Talmud it says, find thyself a teacher. I think I have. . . ."

"We'll see," said Tommy. "Soon enough, we'll see."

The next day, they tried again hunting for

grouse. Tommy had loved the way Avram had prepared the previous day's catch, and insisted they hunt some more. "I'll let you do the shootin' this time," he had promised, and though Avram found this no particular inducement, he'd nevertheless consented.

Tommy rose from the grass and came running toward where Avram lay crouched. "Ya!" he yelled. "Whoopee! Hey! Yaa!" Thirty yards away, a brown-feathered bird rustled through the brush, then suddenly flapped its wings. Avram stood up, aimed as Tommy had shown him, and sighted on the bird. The problem was that the grouse, instead of taking off cleanly, merely fluttered along near the ground. Avram was confused. He fired wildly.

"Hey!" yelled Tommy. "Hey! Hold it up, there! Hold it!" Slowly, he came forward, holding the coat he had used to beat the grass. Along the back were holes from two dozen shotgun pellets.

A teacher I got, thought Avram. The question: Will he live through having me for a pupil?

• • •

Below them, in the canyon, the Laramie River etched a winding path through the mountains of Wyoming. Tommy and Avram rested on their horses, staring down fifty feet at the rushing water.

"The Arapaho say one drink from that river lets a man satisfy a hundred women," said Tommy.

"Is that all at once, or consecutively?" asked Avram.

Tommy shrugged. "Never did find out," he answered.

"I would imagine it's an important distinction," said Avram.

"Have to agree with ya there," said Tommy. He turned his horse back along the edge of the cliff.

"Where are you going?"

"This bends around east a few miles, then comes down where we can cross."

"Why not here?" asked Avram.

Tommy grinned. He wondered if Avram suspected that they'd gone nearly twenty miles out of their way to avoid Fort Laramie. Looking like a medieval castle rising from the hills, Laramie had stone turrets, battlements, carefully placed firing holes, and a full garrison of seasoned troops. One of the principal rest stops on the route to California, Oregon and Utah, the army register of 1850 showed nearly 40,000 men, 2500 women, 25,000 horses, 35,000 oxen and 10,000 wagons, all on their way west. Which was exactly what Tommy wanted to avoid. He was, after all, a wanted man. A description and sketch of him had been circulated and a reward offered. What more likely place than a fort to find himself suddenly recognized? Why, there were probably people there whom he had personally robbed! And so he had taken a detour—kept the fort out of sight and avoided questions.

"*Here* is a good place to die," he said now to Avram, "but not to cross the river."

"Why?" said Avram. "We could just jump down."

"And then what?"

"Swim across. Simple." Avram peered at the rushing water below.

"You-all wanna go kill yourself," said Tommy, "go ahead. I don't like the odds. I'm taking the long way." He moved his horse back along the narrow trail, pressing close to the side of the mountain and away from the edge of the cliff.

Avram stubbornly went on staring down at the river, measuring, gauging. It seemed to him that a jump wouldn't be that bad, that he could make it . . . but finally, he deferred to Tommy's experience. When you had an expert's opinion, you followed it. There was a difference between bravery and foolhardiness. Reluctantly, Avram turned Nuchshlepper away from the precipice and down the path. Before he could swing completely around, however, a rattlesnake scuttled out from under a large rock and flashed through the air at Nuchshlepper's right hind leg. A fang broke off as it struck an iron shoe, but the horse reared in surprise and fright, skidded on some loose gravel, and fell sideways over the cliff.

In the air, struggling to free his feet from the stirrups Avram screamed. "Oy! Oy, gevaaaaa-llllllt!" Down and down he plunged, stuck in the saddle, thinking: To have let me come so far and now to kill me—this isn't right. He hit the water with a huge splash, felt icy pain race through his body. *I—impossible!* he thought. *If I'm in pain, I must still be alive.*

Nuchshlepper, having roughly similar feelings, was swimming frantically for the opposite shore. "I'm alive!" said Avram aloud. "Alive!"

Already, the pain was receding. Actually, it had been shock rather than any serious damage. He was wet, but no more so than when he'd been soaked by rains in Ohio. Even before Nuchshlepper hauled them up on the sloping bank, even before he whinnied and shook the droplets of water from his skin, Avram had bent his head to intone a special prayer. "When I behold Thy heavens, the work of Thy fingers, The moon and the stars which Thou hast established, What is frail man that Thou art mindful of him?" Shiverin but uncaring, Avram began to weep. "Yet Thou hast made him but little less than divine, And dost crown him with glory and majesty."

On the cliff, Tommy watched Avram on the far shore. "Hey!" he yelled, but there was no response. He saw Avram bent in prayer, and figured he had probably injured his neck. Still, he was alive, and appeared to be in one piece. Tommy's pride began to surface. "Son of a bitch!" he said aloud. If he can do it . . .

He backed up a few feet, spurred his horse to a running start, then sailed off into the thin mountain air. "Shee-eee-eee—iiiit!" he yelled as the river hurtled up to meet him. For a moment he and his horse were submerged; then, gasping, they broke the surface. Tommy's hat was missing, and he blew water from his mouth and nose. "Damn!" he said. "Gol-damn!" He saw Avram waving to him from the shore.

"Nice jump!" called Avram.

"You crazy bastard!" yelled Tommy. He felt

solid ground come up beneath him, but did not allow relief to show on his face.

"Remember," said Avram, when Tommy had drawn close enough to hear. "I'm the kind of person, when he says he's going to do something, he does it."

Tommy squeezed some water out of his hair. "I know a lotta them kind of people," he said in mock irritation. "Most of 'em is in the nuthouse or the graveyard." Then, after a moment, he grinned. "Way we're goin', I 'xpect we'll end up in both."

• • •

The families stood watching as gangs of men worked on San Francisco's second post office. The first one was constantly mobbed, swarmed over by hundreds of people throughout the day, people desperate for news of home, or money, or ship tickets to take them away. Wheelbarrows, lumber, and hand tools were scattered about. It was almost the lunch hour and women were already putting out plates of sandwiches and pitchers of beer. Some of the younger girls flirted with the workmen, while small children tried to play in the building area and were shoved away. The structure itself would be single-story, with a pointed, decoratively curved roof and a white façade. Two of the four white pillars had already been erected.

Bialik shielded his eyes from the noonday sun.

"So finally you saw him?" asked Bender.

"After an hour," said Bialik. He'd been appointed as local representative to San Jose, the state capital where Senator William Gwin had established temporary headquarters.

"And?" said Rosensheine.

"And nothing," said Bialik. "He was furious. The vote is off for at least a month. Again, the dopes in Congress can't decide one way or the other."

"Bastards," said Rosensheine. "We're here in anarchy and all they think about is running home to get reelected."

"Anyway," said Bialik, "Gwin told me he definitely would not recommend any change in the state constitution. The South wants slave states, let them make New Mexico or Utah."

"And Fremont?" asked Bender. Fremont was the other senator—though the United States Congress still hadn't accepted California as a state.

"Fremont agrees."

"What about Burnett?" Burnett was the newly elected governor.

"Also."

Bialik sighed. "So we wait, that's all. It'll happen." He looked significantly at Bender. "Of course, about certain other things, I'm not so sure."

"HE'LL BE HERE!" pronounced Bender immediately.

"Says you," commented Rosensheine.

"Don't talk about it, you'll give him a *kinehora*. I'm telling you, he'll be here."

Bialik raised his eyebrows. "A guarantee you got, maybe?"

126

"I got the same guarantee you got from Gwin."

"He could be lying dead—"

"Please!"

"—somewhere in the wilderness. I mean he wasn't on the President Washington. Who knows what could have happened?"

Bender rolled his eyes. "Will you bite your tongue, Bialik? Will you nosh on it? You're talking about my future son-in-law."

"Maybe," said Bialik, pointing, "somebody should remind Sarah Mindl."

Bender followed the line of Bialik's finger. It led to a saw horse table, behind which stood his plump eldest daughter and Julius Rosensheine. The boy was helping himself to another ladle of water from the bucket Sarah Mindl was holding. Even at that distance it was obvious they were flirting. There were constant eye movements, hand touchings, and coy postures. Bender looked back at Herschel Rosensheine, the father. "You had a talk with him?"

Rosensheine stiffened. "A talk? One? I talk to him constantly. It's like reasoning with the ocean."

"But you've explained she's promised to the rabbi? You've laid it out for him?"

"Laid it out, rolled it up, laid it out again. He has certain urges and certain beliefs. What can I do?"

"Tell him to take his urges elsewhere, that's what!" exploded Bender. "And his beliefs!" He strode over to Rosalie, who was helping to set a makeshift table. Through clenched teeth he said, "I want you to get your sister away from that fool."

Rosalie kept working, her eyes averted. "I'm not mixing in."

"Mix, you hear!" said Bender. "I order you! Mix in and do what I say."

"No," said Rosalie quietly.

Bender found her calmness even more irritating than her attitude. "You know who is talking to you?"

"Yes."

"Then maybe you can tell me why God gave me two daughters with such big mouths?"

Rosalie met his gaze. "Because you were born with such small ears."

"Don't you make fun of me," growled Bender, his face reddening. "Don't you make a mockery of your father!" He raised his right hand as if to strike.

"Hit me in public and I'll fall down and scream," said Rosalie quickly. "I'll make the loudest sound you ever heard in your life."

Bender glanced around to see if Bialik and Rosensheine were watching. They were. "This is what it means to be a Yankee?" he asked.

"That's right, Papa."

Bender looked at the sky, then down at Julius and Sarah Mindl. Suddenly he ran toward them, screaming. "Get away from him! Get away! I get my hands on that *pasgudnik*, I'll strangle him! Get away, away. . . ."

Julius gave Sarah Mindl a quick peck on the

128

forehead, then fled toward the rear of the new post office.

"Lunch is ready!" called out Rosalie, with what, under the circumstances, seemed like excessive cheer.

(7)

They made camp five miles from the continental divide.

Tommy had his sewing kit out and was working on one of Avram's boots. With an awl he punched several holes into a flapping piece of leather. "I was, maybe, nineteen when I first camped here," he said. In the distance, the Rockies loomed majestically, an immense and awesome barrier.

"You must have been terrified," said Avram. He reached for the Torah, which he'd carefully double-wrapped in a yellow poncho.

"Too dumb to be scared," said Tommy.

"But you were alone?"

"Yeah. But that didn't bother me none. I was used to bein' alone. Still am." He looked quickly at Avram. "Not that I don't like some company now an' then."

Avram extracted the Torah from its velvet cover and rolled open the scroll. "Well, I'll be damned. . . ." Tommy said.

"Why is that?" asked Avram.

"Well, all this time, I was figurin' you had two bars of gold in there."

"Gold?" Avram chuckled. "Why?"

"Well, the way you take care of it, keepin' it close to you, always brushin' it off, even huggin' it in your sleep all night . . ."

"There are other precious things besides gold."

"True 'nuf," said Tommy. "Which is why I even started thinkin' that maybe you had a girl in there, a little midget one that you made love to when I weren't lookin'. But I never figured that's what it was. . . ." He looked quizzically at the unfurled parchment. "What is it?"

"The Torah," said Avram.

"What's that?"

"Well," said Avram. "It means 'The Teaching'. It's actually the Pentateuch, the Five Books of Moses. Genesis, Exodus, Leviticus, Numbers, and Deuteronomy."

"Sounds familiar," said Tommy.

"There are those who say that the Torah existed in heaven not only before God revealed it to Moses but before He made the earth."

"No shee-it?"said Tommy, craning his neck to see more of the scroll.

"They believe that God made the world by using the Torah for a guide, the way an architect does with a blueprint."

"Amazin' "...

"They say the Torah was written not on parchment then, since nothing existed, but rather in black fire, with white fire as a background."

Tommy stared at the sky. "Tell ya," he said after a moment, "I don't know nothin' about that sort of stuff. I come from Georgia."

Avram edged over and carefully handed the heavy scrolls to Tommy, who held them awkwardly. "What kinda writin' is that?" he asked.

"Hebrew," said Avram.

"Let me hear some."

Avram read a brief passage, then looked up at Tommy's uncomprehending face.

"Try English," said Tommy.

Avram nodded and smiled faintly. "In the beginning," he read, "God created the heaven and the earth. And the earth was without form, and void; and darkness was upon the face of the deep. And the Spirit of God moved upon the face of the waters. And God said, Let there be light: And there was light. And God saw—"

"Whoa!" said Tommy. "Hey, wait jus' a dang—I know that story. That's the reg'lar Bible there." He narrowed his eyes. "Don't go tellin' me Jew folks stole their Torah from the Bible, now. I find that hard to swaller."

"No stealing," said Avram. "The Old Testament is used by Christians and Jews alike. The Jews, as you must know, had it originally. Gentiles have simply added a portion that we don't accept."

"You mean about Christ..."

"Yes."

"Read more."

133

Avram read about Adam and Eve, Cain and Abel, and the Tower of Babel. He read about Abraham, Isaac and Jacob and then skipped to Exodus and the story of Moses. Finally, he came to the part about Mount Sinai, where God gave Moses the Ten Commandments and the Book of the Covenant.

"I used to have a copy of the Ten Commandments," said Avram. "It was engraved on a silver plate. But some men thought the silver more valuable and important than obeying one of the injunctions that was inscribed. A sad irony."

"I'm not sure I exac'ly follow you," said Tommy.

"The eighth commandment is, Thou shalt not steal," explained Avram. "Only they stole it, along with the other nine."

Tommy nodded. "Some folks b'lieve there's a hell of a lot worse things a man can do than steal."

"No doubt," said Avram philosophically. He continued to read, interrupted occasionally by Tommy's hesitant questions, skipping those portions he felt were less interesting than others, or that dwelt on names or technicalities, or that were repetitious. He worked his way gradually through Leviticus and then into Numbers. Several times he looked up and saw that Tommy's face was transfixed, mesmerized like that of a child. And quite unexpectedly, sitting there, in a strange, wild country under a frigid, pitch-black dome of stars, reading the Torah to a Gentile man before a low, crackling camp fire, Avram felt happier than he had ever been.

• • •

The settlement of Stinking Creek was too small to be called a town, too mean and crude even to qualify as a village. It was a kind of stop-off point for travelers on their way north and west, people weary from the endless trek over the Great Plains, or people having second thoughts about going to California and considering the possibility of heading for Oregon. The main street of Stinking Creek was covered with mud. The only wooden structures were the saloon, a general store, a small hotel, and a stable; the rest were tents of canvas, of blankets, of old shirts, or improvised shelters made of thatched weeds and empty barrels, or hovels constructed of large stones and patched with clay. A strong rain could wash half of Stinking Creek away—and frequently did.

Into this charming settlement rode Tommy and Avram, seeking provisions and a night's relief from camping outdoors. They dismounted and tied their horses to a hitching post in front of the hotel.

"Lemme check inside to see what their rates are," said Tommy.

"I have no money," said Avram.

"Well, then I'll ask for their cheapest room," said Tommy. He disappeared through the front door.

Avram would have followed had not his attention been distracted by four men on the opposite side of the street. One of the men was short and stooped with a bowler hat and thick glasses. The three others . . . were familiar. Slow-

135

ly, Avram walked toward them. So intent was he that a passing wagon almost ran him down; the driver cursed at him for his clumsiness, but Avram did not hear. As he drew closer, he heard the man in the bowler speaking in heavily accented English, and saw him slowly withdraw a wallet from a front pocket.

"Hello, hello!" called Avram. "You, hello!"

The men stopped their conversation and looked up. The ones Avram had recognized—the Diggs brothers and Mr. Jones—showed no sign of remembering him. Avram took the foreigner by the arm and led him a few steps away. "I have to warn you," he said with quiet urgency.

"Varn?" said the immigrant. "Vat varn?"

"*Sprechen sie Deutsch?*"

The man's face lit up. "*Ja, ja, ich bin ein Deutscher.*"

"*Sehr gut*," said Avram. He glanced nervously at the three onlookers, then continued in German. "These men are thieves, cutthroats."

"Ya?" said the immigrant. "No. Not so."

"They want only to rob you."

"But . . . they have had a terrible misfortune. They said—"

"I will tell you what they said," interrupted Avram. "Their mother is dying, and they need money to buy back a wagon from the other man."

The immigrant's face sagged. His jaw fell open.

"They said she is in San Francisco—"

"Salt Lake . . ." the immigrant said.

"With me it was San Francisco. They look to you like Mormons?"

136

The immigrant tightened his lips.

"Please," said Avram. "Believe me. They are bad men, dishonest men. Tell them to go away. Just tell them. They're *gonifs*, thieves."

The immigrant looked once at the Diggs brothers, then back at Avram. "Thank you," he said. He began to back away. As the three other men approached, he broke into a run.

Avram stepped forward to intercept the robbers. "Now you don't get him, like you did me."

"Wait a minute, mister," said Darryll.

"Too late," said Arvam.

"We was in the midst of a friendly conversation. . . ."

Mr. Jones pushed Darryll aside. "Who is this pissant?"

Matt, who'd been staring at Avram intently, suddenly raised a hand. "It's comin to me . . . wait a minute . . . it's comin' . . ."

"I want my money," said Avram firmly.

"Ain't you the one . . ." Matt looked at the sky. "Philly! Now I got it. Right off the damn boat."

"And I also want the silver plate you took from me," said Avram.

"What the hell you talkin' about?" said Jones.

Matt stepped between Jones and Avram.

"You hear me, *momser*?" said Avram. "I want what you stole from me. *"Oysvorf*, you. *Parech.*"

"What'd you say to the Dutchie?"

"I cast some doubt on your reliability," said Avram.

"What?"

137

"I told him you were crooks."

Muscles bunched high on Matt's cheeks. "You're bad for business," he said. Without warning, he brought up his fist, smashing into Avram's jaw. Avram responded by reeling backward across the street, stopping only when he bumped into the rear end of Nuchshlepper. Gingerly, he felt his mouth; his hand came away wet with his own blood.

"You see what he did?" he said to Nuchshlepper. Overcome with rage, he charged back at Matt, fists windmilling.

Matt waited until Avram was almost upon him, then leaned sideways and stuck out his left foot, which Avram duly tripped over. As he fell forward, Jones came up to knee him in the stomach, then rabbit-punched him twice in the back of the neck. As Avram sank to his knees, Matt ran behind him and stomped him viciously in the back, sending him sprawling into the mud.

Darryll grabbed a handful of Avram's hair, pulled his head up, and studied his face. Solemnly, he removed his hat. "This man has gone to sleep on us," he announced. "Right here in broad daylight. Just up and nodded off." He let Avram's head fall back into the mud. "I believe our work's about done now," he added.

He walked slowly toward where they had left the wagon. Matt and Jones followed.

● ● ●

Avram came languidly to the surface. He'd been lying peacefully at the bottom of a black pool, the gentle currents slowly swirling around him, when suddenly his body had grown lighter and he had begun to rise. Dim light filtered through his eyelids, and a soft voice let him know that he'd returned to the world of the conscious.

" . . . now. C'mon. C'mon now, ol' buddy."

Avram's lids fluttered open.

"Tha's it. You okay now?"

Avram felt straw against his arm. He looked around. He was lying in some kind of stall. Tommy's face hovered above him. A candle provided the only light.

"Hotel didn't have no more rooms," said Tommy, "so I booked us here in the stable. Rates were very reasonable."

Avram moaned. Gingerly, he touched his jaw and felt a wet piece of cloth. He ran his hand down his cheeks and over an assortment of swellings.

"Some miners tol' me what happened," said Tommy. "Said you took on the three of 'em."

"I took on no one," said Avram. "I only asked them to return what is mine."

"How old is the younger brother?" asked Tommy softly.

Avram felt a dull ache near his kidneys. "About forty, I think. Maybe forty-five."

"And this 'Mr. Jones'?"

Avram grunted. "I don't know. Older. Maybe fifty, fifty-five."

"They sure give you a goin' over."

"Maybe they don't care for Jews," said Avram.

"How big is the big one?"

"Big enough," said Avram. "Why? What difference does it make?"

139

"Big difference," said Tommy. "I may have to shoot that one."

Avram sat up. "I don't want any killing."

"Sometimes you don't have a choice."

"There is always a choice," said Avram. "Sometimes it's more difficult than others, that's all."

"This one is easy," said Tommy.

"Yes it is," said Avram. "You recall the Ten Commandments I read to you?"

"I do. I heerd 'em before."

"Hearing them and living by them are two different things," said Avram, regretting the pompous way in which his words seemed to be coming out, yet not quite able to stop himself. "One of the Commandments says, Thou shalt not kill. My choice, therefore, is not to have any killing."

"Would you rather they killed you?" asked Tommy.

Avram, anticipating the question, snapped a reply. "Life is very simple for you, isn't it?"

"That's funny," said Tommy, "I was just thinking the same thing about you."

Avram leaned back, the full extent of his injuries and fatigue just beginning to make themselves felt. He had never thought much about his body, assuming subconsciously that it could, more or less, stand unlimited abuse—nearly anything short of death or broken bones—without seriously inconveniencing him. Now he suspected otherwise.

"If you don't mind," he said, "I'd like to relax a couple of hours. What time is it, by the way?"

"'Bout midnight, I reckon," said Tommy.

"Midnight! Midnight?"

Tommy grinned. "You was out maybe eight, nine hours, buddy. Plumb stone cold. I was beginnin' to think you intended to sleep permanent."

"Such luxury I can't afford," said Avram. "Wake me at sun-up. If I moan, give me five more minutes." He laid his head back in the straw.

Tommy still sat erect. "Now, look here, Cuz," he said slowly. "You ain' looked outside the las' few hours. This isn't travelin' weather."

"The weather is the weather," said Avram, "and traveling is traveling. I lived up to now, I'll live a little longer. I have a commitment."

"Look," said Tommy reasonably, "I know this place ain't fancy, but it has a roof . . . and it's cheap. We'll hole up here for a spell an' then head south in a week or two."

"No."

Tommy stared at the ceiling for several seconds before looking down. "When you fell on your head you must've mushed your brains."

"My brain is fine, thank you," said Avram. "A little swollen maybe, but functioning as well as ever."

"Listen," said Tommy, "if you're so god-damned worried about time, how come you don't ride on Saturdays?"

"I told you, it's against my religion to ride on the Sabbath."

Tommy shook his head. "Well, I got me a new religion."

"Newer, yes," said Avram. "Better . . . ?" He shrugged. "It's not an unusual disagreement."

141

"Well, in my religion," said Tommy, "one of the things we ain't allowed to do is die."

"You have my great good wishes," said Avram.

"I'm tellin' you we can't make it. I been askin' around."

"We'll make it," said Avram. "Don't ask."

"You don' unnerstand. Them's real mountains, with only certain ways you can get through. An' this is a blizzard comin' up."

"We can make it," stated Avram flatly.

"We? *We?* You an' who?"

"If not you, then Nuchshlepper and I."

"That . . . that sad ol' bag of rotten bones, that thing you ride that looks more like a donkey than a—"

"Please," said Avram. "He may hear you."

Tommy banged his fist on the side of the stall. "Goddamnit! I ain't gonna let you talk me into this!"

"That's entirely up to you."

"What you wanna do is *im*possible. You hear? Impossible. Every goddamn Indian knows that. Every goddamn trapper knows that."

Avram stared pointedly.

"I . . . I'm sorry," said Tommy. "I know you don't like it when I . . ."

Avram shrugged. "You are who you are. And I guess the same is true for me."

"It's just . . . you ain't gonna talk me inta this one," said Tommy. "Until now . . . well, sometimes I'd wake up at night an' I'd look up at the sky an' I'd ask myself what the hell am I doin' here . . . an' I'd say, Well, what else you got to do that's any better? But this time I got me a answer. It's better to keep livin' than to die. An' I aim to die old."

"I wouldn't wish you anything else," said Avram.

"Ah!" said Tommy, exasperated. He crossed to the other end of the stall and lay down on the straw. "Goodbye, Cuz!" he called. "Have a good trip."

"Goodbye," said Avram. "And thank you for everything. You are a good person, a great person, and I will never be able to repay you for your kindness. May God watch over you." He sat up again to take a final look at his friend.

Tommy, however, had turned his face away. "Don't wake me in the morning."

"I'll be quiet as the snow."

"You'll be buried in the snow!"

"Sleep well, my friend."

Tommy put his hat over his face. "You stupid, Jewish, stubborn, sonofabitch, cockeyed bastard."

"Pardon?" said Avram.

Tommy removed the hat. "I said, good luck."

"Thank you."

Avram blew out the candle. And so we part now, he thought. And if you are right, and it's God's will that I perish, then so be it. You have taken me far, my friend, but there comes a time when a man must go into the world alone, and now is that time.

He lay back. When he awoke in the morning, Tommy had already saddled the horses.

• • •

(8)

The history of journeys over the Rocky Mountains is the history of its passes. Their names are inextricably linked with the great explorers of the American continent: Coronado crossing LaGlorieta in 1540; Zebulon Pike descending through Medano Pass; David Thompson finding Athabasca at the north edge of the Columbia Ice Field; Price Hunt reaching the top of Powder River Pass after coming from Crazy Woman Creek in 1811. Perhaps the greatest of the passes, however, is so wide as to scarcely deserve the name. Where the others are mere slots in the huge mountain barriers, South Pass is a complete break in the Rockies chain. Eighteen miles wide, it is the only location in 2000 miles of Rocky Mountains where you can cross without climbing anything and with a reasonable chance of not dying of thirst.

Unfortunately for white, westbound immigrants, Indians knew this first.

Tommy bent down and examined the remains. They lay amidst the charred frames of their wagons—two entire families, as best he could judge. Nine people in all, every one scalped, some with limbs hacked off, others with fingers still clenched around arrows that had entered their bodies. Even the oxen had been slain; already the stench from their carcasses was overpowering.

"Crow, I'd say," said Tommy, remounting. "They got no use for oxen."

"It was slaughter," said Avram, stunned.

"Yep."

"Hideous."

"Yep. Ain't that unusual, either. People die like flies aroun' here. I heerd once that two people drown each day just tryin' to cross the North Platte. It's rough country."

"Come," said Avram. "We may as well go."

Tommy, unmoving, shook his head. "Not that way, we're not. The Indians done this are still aroun'. Waitin' is my guess. We head direc' through the pass, you an' me gonna get a close haircut, jus' like these folks here."

"What would you suggest, then?"

"Head back."

"Besides that."

Tommy scratched his head. "Well, le's see. That big butte south of here is Continental Peak. Crow'll git us afore we come within' a mile of it. North, you got the Wind River Range, which is jus' about the bigges' mountains in the world. We could stay east of them, maybe foller the Wind River, git us up to Union Pass."

"How long would that take?" asked Avram.

"Couple weeks. We'd probably freeze to death on the way, though."

"And so what's the alternative?"

"It's risky."

"Everything is risky."

"Well, then, okay. The Sweetwater River—that stream we crossed a mile back—that cuts a path up into them tall peaks. A little west of it is the Little Sandy Creek. My own personal opinion, when I used to trap around these parts, was that somewhere in the mountains there ought to be a passable piece of land connectin' those two." He paused. " 'Course, I never ackshully found it."

Avram swung his horse around. "Let's look again," he said brightly.

• • •

It was snowing. Or it was hailing. Or it was pouring freezing rain. The exact nature of the precipitation changed from minute to minute. Only the howling wind remained constant, driving whatever it was that fell from the sky full force into their faces. They were heading upwards now after following the Sweetwater for as long as they could. In the distance towered Wind River Peak, 13,000 feet high. Avram, wrapped in blankets, had tied a scarf over his hat and under his chin.

Tommy, leading the way, yelled back, "What do you think, Cuz?"

"Freezing."

"Damn right it is. Colder'n a witch's teat."

"Colder even than Cracow," said Avram.

"You should see it in winter," said Tommy.

A day later they were above the tree line, skirting the side of the mountain in search of a pass that perhaps did not exist. The blizzard was now pure snow and had intensified. They walked in front of the horses, pulling them through waist-high drifts, straining to see three feet ahead. Tommy saw Avram begin to wander away.

"Snow blind!" he yelled through the driving gale.

"What?"

Tommy jerked his horse so that it was close to Avram's side. He took Avram's hand and placed it on the horse's tail. "Hang on to this!" he shouted, his voice muffled and half-lost in the icy wind.

They pushed onward, Tommy in the lead. Then, on a patch of steeply sloped ice, he slipped and lost his balance. Letting go the reins, he skidded down the side of the mountain, sliding and rolling, unable to gain a hold. When he finally stopped, he was nearly fifty yards away from Avram and the two horses. It was a twenty minute struggle before he could claw his way back up.

"That's it!" he shouted, when he finally crept alongside his horse.

"What's it?" said Avram.

"That's it! Can't go no further. We're stopping here." He grabbed his horse's reins and jerked sharply downward, forcing the animal to lie in the snow.

"What are you doing?"

"Git your mount down!" Tommy ordered. As he said this, he grabbed Nuchshlepper's reins and forced Avram's horse to the ground. Now the two horses formed an L-shaped barrier against the wind.

Avram tried to pull Nuchshlepper erect.

"Hey!" said Tommy, grabbing him in a bear hug.

"I don't like it here!" shouted Avram. "I think we could find someplace a little more comfortable."

"It's here or nothin'!" shouted Tommy.

"But my commitment . . ."

"If we go on, we die," said Tommy forcefully. "You can't meet your commitment if you're dead, can you?"

Avram considered and realized Tommy was right. "Okay," he said meekly.

"Git the blankets!"

Avram tugged the two bedrolls from the saddles as Tommy knelt in the snow, holding down the two horses. Avram unrolled Tommy's blanket, then started on his own.

"No!" shouted Tommy above the screaming wind. "Make one!"

Avram hesitated.

"Move!"

Avram put the two sets of blankets together and fashioned one large bedroll. Tommy, the horses' reins still in his hands, wriggled inside. "Hop in!" he said.

Avram, doubtful, eased himself between the blankets, careful to leave a space between Tommy and himself.

"Closer," said Tommy.

"We . . . are doing this for warmth, am I correct?" said Avram stiffly.

"Uh-huh . . ."

"In that case," said Avram, "I make you a formal offer—you may put your arms around me."

Tommy grinned. "You're better lookin' than some of them squaws I been with, if that's any comfort to ya."

"I'm afraid," said Avram, "right at this moment, it's not."

"Aw," said Tommy, "come 'ere, darlin'." He enfolded Avram in his arms.

After three hours, both men fell asleep.

• • •

When Avram woke, it took him several seconds before he realized he was alone. He wriggled out of the blankets, brushed himself off, and stood up. It was still snowing very lightly, but the wind had died down and there were patches of sky where stars shone through. Avram saw Nuchshlepper standing quietly nearby. He went over and stroked the horse's head.

"It was a tough time for you," he said. "I realize that."

Nuchshlepper shuddered.

"Believe me," said Avram, "I could use a hot bath myself. Then, a nice bowl of soup with *kreplach*, maybe some bagels, some—" What am I talking? he thought. He reached into one of the

150

saddle bags and came up with a handful of sugar, which he let Nuchshlepper lick off. "So," he said, "now it's just you and me."

Avram looked around at the vast expanses of brutal white on all sides. He shrugged. "You can't blame the man," he said. "He needs me like an attack of cholera. He'll make twice as good time alone."

Looking up, he saw the dark outline of a large bird sail high over the mountain and disappear behind an outcropping of rock. The snow accumulated on Avram's eyelashes and temporarily blurred his vision. "So maybe," he said to Nuchshlepper, "you could learn how to grow wings." He sank back down to the ground. Without benefit of the sun, he had no idea which direction was west. His only option was to wait for daylight.

He had almost dozed off again when a sound came echoing up the side of the mountain, a series of excited whoops. Indians! thought Avram. *I'm finished*. The whoops grew nearer. "Yaahoooo! Whoooeeee! Eeeeeyaaooowie!"

Avram stood up. In the faint, snow-reflected starlight he saw a lone figure on horseback coming slowly in his direction.

"Tommy!"

"Hey, Avram!"

"My God," said Avram slowly. "A miracle."

"I foun' the sumbitch!" yelled Tommy happily. "Less'n two miles away. I foun' the Li'l Sandy!"

But Avram scarcely heard, for by this time he was already lost in prayer.

The next day was one of those sun-washed,

151

ice-clear periods that often seem to follow great storms. The sky was a resplendent blue-violet, depthless and cloudless. Avram and Tommy rode slowly over the rolling, treeless hills of what is now southwest Wyoming and followed the general trail known as the Sublette Cut-off, discovered by William Sublette twenty-six years earlier. From the Little Sandy they crossed west to the Big Sandy, then over to the Green River, up Fontenelle Creek, across the Green River-Bear River divide and into present-day Idaho at the northern portion of Bear Lake. Near the lake shore, Avram saw some scattered abandoned firearms, then articles of clothing and bedding strewn along the ground, buffalo skins, chests, and finally a series of graves.

Tommy shook his head. "Coulda been anythin'. Fever. Indians. Some folks jus' give up. They come two thousan' miles an' then they jus' lay down an' die."

"Terrible," said Avram. "The suffering . . ." He noticed one of the graves had been torn open; a jaw bone with teeth intact lay beside it.

"Wolves," said Tommy. "Rip the dead right up."

Avram, nauseated, turned away. A few hours later, heading north, they discovered a small town just where the Bear River bent around in a U-shaped arc. Although the main street was dirt, there were nevertheless an impressive number of wooden buildings, several boasting two stories. Avram read the signs out front as they trotted past an Episcopal church, a schoolhouse, and then a row of stores: Judd's Meat Market, an Advocate's Office, Overbay's Dry Goods, and

Powell's Saloon. They slowed down just past the barber shop and drew to a halt outside the First Bank of Soda Springs. Tommy dismounted and handed his horse's reins to Avram.

"'Bout time to reprovision, I expect," he said.

"You need some help?" asked Avram. "I could carry—"

"No, no," said Tommy. "I can handle it. You jus' hold the horses."

"We could tie them."

Tommy shook his head. "I'll be two minutes. I got a little business to take care of. You'll see— I'll be right out." He walked into the bank and disappeared through the doors.

Avram reached into his coat and removed a crust of bread. Actually, they still had a substantial amount of food left, but perhaps Tommy was being prudent. He had mentioned that they would soon turn back south and reach the beginning of the California Trail. Possibly, provisioning themselves now would permit them to gain a swift start and avoid wasting time in the future. Avram gnawed hungrily at the crust.

Inside the bank, Tommy had sidled casually up to one of the teller's windows.

"Can I help you, young man?" said the elderly woman inside the cage.

"I believe so, m'am," said Tommy, "if you all would jus' be willin' to wait a minute."

The woman smiled.

Tommy whirled and drew both of his revolvers. He instantly surveyed the seven people in the bank; then, in a loud but calm voice, he said, "I want you all to relax an' listen to me, because I'm only gonna say this once."

Immediately, four of the men raised their hands, as did two of the women. The fifth man, a gangling, mean-looking fellow with curly, uncombed hair, kept his arms by his sides.

"There's a man behind you with a big shotgun," Tommy said, "but don't turn around."

The curly-haired man twisted his neck very slightly.

"I'm warnin' you," said Tommy. "He don't care to be recognized."

"How we know you tellin' the truth?" said Curly.

"Turn aroun'," said Tommy, grinning. "If you feel your head gittin' blowed away, then you know I weren't lyin'."

The man stiffened.

"Good," said Tommy. "Now slowly, everybody put your hands on top of your head." He lowered his voice and leaned backwards toward the teller. "'Ceptin' you, sweetcakes. You jus' fill up one a them canvas bags with all the money you have." He waited while the woman stood paralyzed. "Move it!"

The teller slid open a drawer in front of her and began withdrawing coins and bills. The curly-haired man was studying Tommy's face.

"You part of the McGargle bunch?" he asked.

"Could be," said Tommy.

"You're gonna pay for this," said the man. "I'm the one who got McGargle's partner, you know."

"That right?" said Tommy, not eager to correct the misidentification. "We was wonderin' . . ."

"Tied him to a post an' used him for target practice. One of m' deputies still carries his ear as a watch fob." He paused. " 'Less you put down them guns, same thing's gonna happen to you, boy."

Tommy squinted, making his face as hard-looking as he could. "You the law here? What's your name, mister?"

"Luke Daniels," said the man. "And you best remember it."

From the corner of his eye Tommy saw that one canvas bag was nearly filled with cash. "Jus' hand it over, dumplin'," he said to the teller. "Nice an' easy." He reached back and the woman hooked the bag's drawstrings over the end of his pistol. "Thank you, li'l bird," said Tommy as he moved toward the door. He stopped near Daniels, who scowled at him.

"Remember," said Daniels.

"Oh, I will," said Tommy. "An' here's somethin' to aid your own recall." With that, he slammed the barrel of one gun into Daniels's cheek and watched him stagger, then sink to his knees. "Don't fergit!" he shouted to the others. "My partner is coverin' me outside, so don't turn aroun' for at least five minutes."

He burst out the doors of the bank, holstered his guns, and raced for the horses. Avram turned just as Tommy stuffed the canvas bag into his poncho.

"You know," said Avram, "I've been looking at that restaurant across the street. They do a nice little business. Why don't we treat ourselves to a hot meal?"

155

"I don't think so," said Tommy. He whacked Avram's horse on the rump and spurred his own mount. Both animals lurched forward.

"Hey, wh—"

"Git your ass movin'!" shouted Tommy. Side by side, they galloped down the street.

"What happened?" yelled Avram, clinging frantically to Nuchshlepper's back.

"We jus' robbed us a bank!"

"We *what*? What do you mean, *we*?"

From behind them came a tremendous explosion. Tommy glanced around, saw Daniels, his head bleeding, beginning to reload a shotgun. Tommy drew one of his pistols and fired, driving Daniels back indoors. The gun Tommy employed was a Colt single-action forty-five that he had modified to function using only the hammer. He would curl his thumb to pull the hammer back, then let it spring forward—it was quicker and more accurate than squeezing a trigger. In rapid order, he pegged four more shots in the bank's general direction, then turned and jabbed his heels into his horse's sides. "That'll hold 'em," he yelled.

"You maniac!" screamed Avram.

Two minutes later, cautiously this time, Daniels again emerged into the street. "The bank!" he shouted. "They robbed the bank!"

From other buildings, a few men and women began to appear.

"We need a posse, boys," said Daniels. "Let's go!"

More men came into the street.

"Boys!" said Daniels, glowering at the crowd. "I said . . . *we need a posse!*"

"Fuck you," called out a weasly-looking fellow.

"Didn't you hear?" said Daniels. "They just robbed the bank."

"I ain't got no money in the bank."

"But they robbed it!"

"Well, go git 'em," said another man. "It's your bank. Besides which, you're the sheriff."

"How 'bout you, Billy?" said Daniels, looking over at a teenager wearing suspenders.

"I ain't goin' out there," came the answer.

"Sam?" said Daniels, turning to another, frail-looking, man.

"Not today," said Sam. "I have a lot of loose change in my pockets, and I'm afraid if I ride my horse it'll fall out."

"Tightwad!" sneered Daniels. He drew himself up to his full height and ran a gnarled hand through impossibly curly hair. "All right, you puss-pimpled hooker's sores!" At this, several women retreated back indoors. "Five dollars a man when we catch 'em."

No one stepped forward.

"Seven-fifty!"

Still no volunteers.

"I'll go fer ten," said Sam. "Even if I lose m' change, it's worth it."

"All right, you skunk suckers!" shouted Daniels. "Ten dollars a man. Ten!"

Eight men came forward.

"I get their ears," said Daniels hoarsely. "Just you all remember that."

● ● ●

Avram and Tommy stopped for a moment on a high bluff and surveyed the scene down below. Billows of dust from the pursuing horsemen were clearly visible.

"We'd better git goin'," said Tommy.

"How could you do this?" said Avram.

"Easy," said Tommy. "It's what I do fer a livin'."

"But you made me an accomplice! An associate!"

"I wouldn't exac'ly call you an associate," said Tommy blithely. "More like an apprentice, I'd say. You gotta work up to bein' an associate. Learn the business."

Avram scarcely heard him. He was furious. "You made me a bank robber!"

"So what?" said Tommy. "You'll git your half."

Avram, frustrated beyond all reason and restraint, screamed with anger, then leaped from his saddle and flew at Tommy. His momentum carried both of them to the ground, where they rolled over and over, Avram pummeling Tommy with his fists.

"*Gonif!*" screamed Avram. "Maniac! No-goodnik! *Momser!*"

Tommy tried to defend himself rather than hit back, but Avram could not be fought off. Finally, with a mighty shove, Tommy managed to create a foot-long gap between them. Unfortunately for him, at exactly this instant Avram let go with a wild, roundhouse right that caught Tommy flush on the nose. He staggered backward and fell, blood gushing from both nostrils. When he stood up, he had a gun in each hand.

"Guns?" shouted Avram. "You're going to use a gun on me?"

Tommy cocked his head slightly.

"You bastard, you!" screamed Avram. *"Graubyon!"*

"Don't call me no grub-yon," said Tommy.

But Avram, despite the guns, was already charging head first, like an enraged bull. It was a relatively simple matter for Tommy to sidestep and bring one of the gun barrels down hard on Avram's left temple. Avram collapsed. Tommy holstered his pistols.

Two minutes later, Avram stirred. Dazedly, he raised himself to a sitting posture. The men stared at each other in silence. Tommy wiped the blood from his nose and mouth.

"You know, you're crazy," he said.

Avram nodded. "Of course, I'm crazy. I'm a bank robber."

"Oh, come on . . ."

"Who else would rob a bank but a *meshuggene?"*

"You ain't no bank robber."

"No? Then how come I'm running? Why did someone shoot at me and why am I being chased?"

"Aw, come on now," said Tommy. "All you done was hold the horses."

"You think I could go back and explain that to them?" said Avram. He carefully probed the area above his temple where the pistol had struck him. A shaft of pain knifed through his head.

"Sure, you can go back," said Tommy.

"Will they listen?"

"Yeah, they'll listen."

Avram stood up. "Then I think I'll try it."

"An' after they're done listenin' they'll hang you."

Reflexively, Avram touched his adam's apple. "What if I gave them back the money?"

"You mean your half."

"Yes. My half."

"Well, first they'll string you up by your privates till you tell 'em where the other half is—"

"I'll explain that you refused to come with me."

"—and *then* they'll hang you."

Avram considered a moment. "I can't believe they would do such a thing."

"Believe it."

"But they're officers of the law."

Tommy grinned. " 'Law' is jus' a word aroun' these parts," he explained. "Those men ain't concerned with the law. They jus' wants some money an' the fun of seein' somebody hang. Hang if you get lucky, that is. I seen one posse string a man up to a telegraph pole, then cut off each finger an' toe separate, one every fifteen minutes. Took that feller a long time to die."

"But—"

" 'Nother time, up near Hangtown, I seen a group of vigilantes—miners they were—catch a Mexican they figured had murdered a white woman. Turned out he wasn't the one, but meantime they held the greaseball's head in a bucket till he drowned." He paused for effect. "Now . . . you wanna go back an' explain how you only watched the horses, you go right on ahead."

Avram looked back at the dust cloud, which was growing steadily larger.

"When we first met," said Tommy, "you knew it was me that robbed that train you was on, didn' you?"

"I suppose," said Avram, "deep down, I knew. But I hadn't seen you directly, and I thought, well, maybe I could be wrong."

"You weren't wrong."

"Now, I know," said Avram. "I also know that one can't close one's eyes to a situation. As a Jew I should've known that long ago, but I guess I needed a new lesson."

"It ain' easy robbin' a train by yourself," said Tommy.

"I'm sure it's not."

"It takes a lotta skill. When I used to work with a partner, he'd cover the engineer and the fireman, an' then throw water into the firebox to kill the engine, an' I'd handle the passengers. Since I been workin' alone it's a lot tougher."

"What—you want my sympathy?" said Avram.

"Right now," said Tommy, looking nervously at the approaching posse, "all I want is fer you to make up your mind."

Avram pressed his lips together, then remounted Nuchshlepper. "How could you do this to me?"

"I'll tell you later," said Tommy.

They began to ride. Avram once more fingered his temple. "Is this what you did to that guy who's chasing us?"

Tommy snickered. "Daniels. Yeah, I buffaloed him good."

"No wonder he's after you."

Tommy touched a finger to the top of his nose. "You know, you're the hardest hitting rabbi I ever come up against."

"Thank you," said Avram solemnly.

• • •

(9)

Thirty minutes after Tommy and Avram had departed the bluff, the posse arrived at that location. Billy, the teenager, dismounted and examined the ground.

"They was here, all right."

Daniels dismounted also, as did another man, a lean, pock-marked, wolfish individual nicknamed Cockeyed Frank. Cockeyed Frank had been an army scout until he was dismissed for giving ambiguous directions. A red splotch caught his eye and he knelt to examine it. "Here's some blood," he said.

"That was me," said Daniels proudly. "I knew I got that one."

"If you did," said Cockeyed Frank, "he sure took a long time to start bleeding."

"You callin' me a liar?" said Daniels, eyes narrowing.

"Jus' lookin' at the possibilities is all," said Cockeyed Frank. "This here could be animal blood. Or maybe you right, maybe they *was* here, but it was days ago."

"Mmm," said Daniels sullenly. "Well, I think we oughta mount up an' just foller them tracks."

Cockeyed Frank dipped two fingers in the blood spot and gingerly touched them to his tongue. Daniels looked on fascinated. "That tell you somethin'?"

Cockeyed Frank shrugged. "Not me. I jus' was innerested in seein' how it tastes, that's all."

Daniels blanched, but kept himself under control. "Moron!" he said. "Get on your horse."

Cockeyed Frank remounted. Actually, the reason he'd sampled the blood was to gauge the temperature. It was still somewhat warm—proof that their quarry was not too distant—but there was no need to tell Daniels everything.

"Let's go, men," said Daniels, waving. "And keep an eye out for a nice tree with low branches. We'll need one fer hangin'."

● ● ●

Tommy headed generally west and south, following close to shallow rivers and creeks so that tracking would be more difficult. It could, of course, work both ways. A flowing body of water obscured hoofprints quite well, but if the same stream dried up, as often happened, the trail would be visible for days, baked into the mud. The gamble had to be taken; the nature of the countryside provided few other means of cover. They eventually made their way into Utah Territory—the part that is now Nevada—avoiding the Great Salt desert and paralleling, one after another, Goose Creek, Salmon Falls Creek, the Mary's River, and finally Maggie Creek in the Tuscarora Mountains. Here Tommy headed three hundred yards down a shallow tributary, then reined to a halt.

"*Nu?*" said Avram. "You're tired?"

"We're doublin' back now," said Tommy. "Pick up the main crick back at the fork."

Avram smiled. "Ah, a trick. I see. Very shrewd."

Tommy shrugged. "Maybe. Maybe not."

"You don't think it'll work?"

"Maybe. Maybe not."

"I wish you could give me a more responsive answer," said Avram. "Can you?"

"Maybe," said Tommy. "Then again—" He smiled. "Depends what kinda tracker they got. A real poor one won' even notice we left the main stream. He'll jus' continue right along, an' so the trick won't work. A real good one will know after a li'l while that we doubled back. So it won't work that way either."

"Our only hope is for a medium-good tracker, then," said Avram.

"You said it, Cuz."

They swung their horses around.

An hour later the posse came to the Maggie Creek tributary. Cockeyed Frank held up a hand for them to stop.

"Which way?" asked Daniels.

Cockeyed Frank dismounted. "Somethin's goin' on here," he said shrewdly.

"Just tell me which way."

Frank peered down into the muddy water, then stooped, rolled up his sleeve, and dipped his hand in until it touched bottom.

"That tell you somethin'?" asked Daniels.

"Nope," said Cockeyed Frank. "Jus' tryin' a wash the blood offa mah fingers from the las' time we stopped."

Daniels drew his gun and cocked the hammer. "You got any more wise-ass answers, you get 'em outa your system now," he said.

"Leave him be," said Sam. "He's our only tracker."

"Some things are more important than even catchin' criminals," sneered Daniels. "And buttoning a bad-ass lip is one of 'em."

"Who's worried about catching anybody?" said Sam. "I'm just concerned we won't be able to find our way home."

As he spoke, Cockeyed Frank spotted a thread dangling from a branch of a tree that overhung the tributary. "They's clever uns, all right," he muttered.

"You trace 'em?" said Daniels.

"Well, way I got it figured," said Frank "is that they purposefully left that thread to make us think they gone down the main stream."

"But the thread is over the feeder," protested Daniels.

"Oh, they knew I'd spot that," said Frank. "That's the trick."

Daniels grinned shrewdly. "So they *really* went down the feeder."

"Or the main stream," said Cockeyed Frank.

Daniels's face quickly hardened and he took careful aim with his pistol.

"Jus' joshin'," said Frank. "Hey, c'mon now, Lucas, can't you take a joke?"

Daniels stared at him stonily.

"They're up the creek," said Cockeyed Frank. "The feeder."

"One of these days I'm gonna see how your head does against a bullet," said Daniels. He holstered his gun. "Let's ride!" he yelled, and the posse resumed the chase.

• • •

They made camp behind some low hills, flanked by freakish-looking extrusions of poorly balanced rock.

"That one there looks like somebody's ear." Munching on a dried biscuit, Tommy pointed to an elliptical, slightly hollow boulder. "I think I'll name it Ear Rock."

Avram huddled miserably near some scrub brush. "I wish we could build a fire. I'm not interested in naming rocks, I'm interested in getting warm."

"No fires," said Tommy. "No tellin' how far behind they is. Come sunrise they'll sure as hell catch on to my dumb-ass trick."

"It's cold," said Avram.

Tommy opened the canvas bag he'd set out in front of him and dumped the contents on the frigid ground. He formed two equal piles, bills and coins, and shoved one of them toward Avram. "Here—this'll warm you up."

Avram just stared.

Tommy began to count. "I make it three hundred twenty dollars each," he said after a while. "That what you git?"

"No," said Avram. "It's not what I get."

Tommy grinned. "Accordin' ta mah figurin', that ain't bad."

Suddenly, Avram snatched up his pile and tucked it into his shirt.

"Well," said Tommy, his grin expanding so that it seemed to take up his entire face, "now ain't that something."

Avram turned away.

"Tell the truth," said Tommy, "I never figured you was ever goin' to take that money, tainted as it is."

"You're misinterpreting things," mumbled Avram.

"Mis—? Well, that's one a them ten dollar words, not that I don't know what it means. But here's another one for ya that's jus' as good an' maybe comes a little closer. *Hy*-pocrisy. You heerd a that one? I learned it from a English teacher I was talkin' to durin' a holdup. Liked it so much I wrote it down. Seems to me that's the key to explainin' the world, right there in that word."

"That's a very one-sided, narrow view," said Avram sullenly.

Tommy nodded. "Maybe," he agreed. "Maybe so. I can only go by what I seen. I look at the sitchuation in this country, 'specially all the feudin' an' fussin' 'bout whether to have slavery in the new territories—an' I say these people is crazy. They quotes the Bible to show how good an' God

168

fearin' they is, an' then they cites the same book to explain how niggers is meant to be slaves. Guess that's why I couldn't never hold with no formal religion. Too much *hy*pocrisy, even though afore that partic'lar robbery I didn't know the word."

"You don't approve of slavery, then?" asked Avram, curious.

"Don't approve or disapprove," said Tommy. "Jus' wish people would quit bullshittin' 'bout the reasons for it, an' tell the truth. 'We strong an' you weak, an' we gonna force you to work for us so's we kin git rich.' That's the reason for slavery. Myself, if I was a nigger, I'd either run away or die tryin'."

Avram made no comment, although he thought sometime in the future he would try to broach the topic of the morality of slavery. It was a mistake, he knew, to imagine that Tommy could not understand such things. He might be rough-hewn and have little formal education, but he was intelligent and independent; it would be a bad error to patronize him.

"Well," said Tommy, "now you're rich. What you gonna do with it?"

Avram looked at him carefully. "When we get to the next town . . . I'm going to send it back."

"That right?"

"Yes. And I hope you would do the same."

"Not likely," said Tommy. "An' mah advice to you is be careful till then. It's dangerous out here. Fella could git hisself robbed." He chuckled heartily.

Avram prepared his bedroll. "With you to

169

protect me," he said, "I'm sure I have nothing to worry about."

The next day, when Tommy awoke, Avram was already at his prayers, facing east and *davening, tallis* draped around his shoulders. Tommy watched for several moments, then took some sugar, biscuits, and dried buffalo meat from his saddlebags. For some time now he had missed having coffee and bacon in the morning, but even in daylight smoke from a fire could be seen from a great distance. He chewed absently on the food, finished in ten minutes, then saddled his horse. Avram was still chanting. Tommy waited impatiently until he saw Avram remove his prayer shawl and begin to fold it.

"Seems to me like you done some extra prayin'," said Tommy. "Guess you figger we gonna need it, huh?"

"There was an extra section today," said Avram, "in addition to the Torah reading. Its called the *Musaf Amidah*. It consists of seven benedictions. You may be interested to know that the first twenty-two words of the middle one have initial letters that follow the Hebrew alphabet, in reverse order." He smiled mischievously.

"Couldn't care less," said Tommy.

"Actually," said Avram. "I suspected that might be the case."

"Anyway," said Tommy, "church is over. Let's make tracks." He lifted up Avram's saddle.

Avram made no move to take it, and Tommy threw it over Nuchshlepper's back. Avram grabbed the horse's reins and began to walk.

"What the hell you doin'?" said Tommy.

170

"You haven't been with me long enough to know?"

Tommy's eyes widened. "Don't tell me you're—" He began to shake his head. "I don' believe this."

"I don't ride today," said Avram.

"What are you talking about?"

"It's Saturday."

"So?"

"I don't ride on Saturday."

"I unnerstan' that. *But don't tell me you ain't gonna ride today.*"

"All right," said Avram. "You don't want to hear, I won't tell you."

"But you ain't gonna ride . . ."

"No."

Tommy punched the air with his fist. "Damn!" He tried to control his voice. "Are you aware this ain't a reg'lar Saturday?"

Avram smiled faintly. "Why is this Saturday different from all other Saturdays?"

" 'Cause on this one there is a fuckin' posse chasin' us."

Avram shrugged. "During the Maccabean revolt there were many Jews who allowed themselves to be killed rather than resist."

"I don't care about what they done in the bean revolt," said Tommy. "All I know is there's a bunch of murderin' lunatics out to stretch our necks, an' they're gittin' meaner an' madder every day."

"They can't do worse than kill us," said Avram.

"You happen to be wrong there," said Tom-

171

my. "But forgit that. If we don' move out now, we're in big trouble."

"Why? That trick you played ought to fool them for a long time. Maybe permanently."

"I promise you," said Tommy, veins standing out in his forehead, "they're doublin' back to that stream right now."

Avram took a deep breath. "I don't ride on Saturday."

"How 'bout dyin' on Saturday? You allowed to do that?"

"Only if it involves no work."

"Jee-sus," said Tommy. He removed his Stetson, slapped it against his thigh. "You give me the peedoodles, you know that? You surely do. You unnerstan' that they ain't no Jews in that posse chasin' us?"

"I realize it's not likely . . ."

"That they'd jus' as soon string you up on Saturday as they would on any other day?"

"It's not my fault they don't observe a holiday," said Avram.

"They don't give a *shit* for your holidays!" shouted Tommy.

Avram continued to shuffle ahead.

"Goddamned if I'm gonna walk," yelled Tommy.

Avram looked back reprovingly. "I've asked you not to say that."

"Oh, but it's okay to say 'fuckin'?"

"One is merely puerile, the other is profane," said Avram. "There's a difference."

"Look, you stupid, ignorant, pure-eel or whatever sonofabitch, *I* ain't waitin' aroun' here for that posse to find us. *I* am leavin'."

172

"Who's asking you to stay?"

Tommy raised his hat. "Goodbye." He galloped off. A moment later he was gone, vanished beyond a nearby hill.

• • •

The posse was back by the fork in Maggie Creek.

"You miserable asshole," said Daniels to the man just in front of him. "No wonder you got drummed outa the army."

"Anyone could've made the same mistake," said Cockeyed Frank. "Don't go cussin' me out jus' because I'm a human bein'."

"You did a slovenly job," said Daniels. "You don't measure up."

"Fuck you," said Frank. "I don't have to take this abuse. I'll seek employment elsewhere." He turned his horse out of the stream.

"Don't expect a good recommendation from me," said Daniels. He watched as Cockeyed Frank rode slowly away. "Hey, Cockeye!" he called.

Frank turned in his saddle.

"Here's your severance pay," said Daniels. He drew his pistol and very slowly and deliberately aimed and fired. The bullet hit Cockeyed Frank in the face.

Daniels looked around. "Anyone else wanna change employment mid-stream?" he asked.

There were no takers.

"Good," said Daniels. "Let's move ahead." Urging his horse forward, he began to calculate. As tracker, Frank was earning fourteen dollars a day, four more than the rest of the posse members. If they were out for another five days, the savings would be seventy dollars. Not bad, thought Daniels. Not bad. After all, a good manager was always on the lookout for economies.

● ● ● ●

The sagebrush extended right down to the banks of the river, the tender tips of fresh spring growth beginning to mingle with the austere winter gray. The river was the Humboldt—although Avram did not know its name—and it straggled through the desert across most of the width of Nevada, providing grass for animals, water for men and beasts, and relief from the endless miles of wind-blown sand. Discovered by the trapper, Peter Ogden, in 1828, it was the principal body of water on the California trail.

Avram let Nuchshlepper graze on the river bank for twenty minutes, then seized the reins and began again to walk. A short time in the arid countryside had clarified his basic strategy: This route was the only way anything living would ever make it farther west. Deception of those following was no longer possible: they simply had to be outrun. He plodded on for another half hour, then detoured around a huge copper-colored boulder. On the other side, Tommy was leaning casually against the rock, munching on a pine nut.

"Care for one?" he said nonchalantly.

Avram's face brightened. He had not realized the absolute desolation of being alone in

174

this vast country. "I . . . I don't think so," he stammered in surprise. "I'm on a diet."

Tommy laughed. "Hey, you know what?"

"What?"

"I've been doin' some figurin'. Today ain't Saturday."

Avram, who had stopped, began again to walk. "I think this trip is driving you mad."

"I swear to God," said Tommy. "It ain't Saturday. It's Friday."

"Then five days ago was Sunday."

"Right."

"We robbed the bank on Sunday?"

"It's possible."

"What year is it?" asked Avram.

"What?"

"You heard me. What is the year?"

"It's eighteen-fifty. What's the—"

"Well, the Jewish year is five thousand six hundred ten," said Avram, "and if we can keep track of that, we can tell what day is Saturday, *chacham*."

Tommy's face reddened. "Git your ass on that horse."

Avram continued walking.

"You hear me? Git on there, an' don't tell me you don't ride on Saturday."

"Sorry," said Avram. "I don't ride on Saturday."

"I asked you not to tell me that!"

Avram shrugged.

Near midday, they turned south, following the river as it wended its way through the Trinity range. Avram trailed Tommy to the top of a hill.

175

"Come 'ere," said Tommy. "Got somethin' I wanna show ya." He pointed down the valley of the Humboldt, back in the direction they'd come from.

"You know what that is?"

Avram squinted. "To me, it looks like a blotch."

"A movin' one, right?"

"Yes."

"It's them."

"All right. So it's them."

"*Well?*"

"When the sun sets, I'll ride. Not before."

Tommy looked up at the bright afternoon sky. Suddenly a flawless argument occurred to him. "I'm gonna show you that you're unreasonable," he said.

"Religion has nothing to do with reason," said Avram. "It's faith. Please . . . don't waste your time. When the sun goes down, I will ride."

"Suppose the sun doesn't go down."

"What? I think—"

"Hear me out. We're travelin' west, right?" said Tommy.

"Yes, but—"

"An' the sun is travelin' west too, right?"

Avram summoned his one directional fact: The sun rises in the east and sets in the west. "Yes . . ." he said tentatively.

Tommy, who'd been slumping in the saddle, straightened triumphantly. "Then we always gonna be underneath the sun 'cause it an' us is both a goin' in the same direction!"

"That's ridiculous."

176

"The sun ain't never gonna set, so you may as well forgit about your Sabbath."

"It will set," said Avram. "We've been traveling west all this time and it's set before. It will set again."

"But now we're goin' faster," pleaded Tommy. "*We's runnin'*, dammit!"

"Please . . ."

"All right, all right. But ain't we?"

"Yes."

"So?"

"When the sun sets."

Tommy puffed out his cheeks. "Man, you stubborner than a hog at a trough full of slops."

"Please . . ."

"Well, can't you allow half a day 'cause we're movin' with the sun?" He looked at Avram, who stared straight ahead. "A quarter?" Tommy tightened his lips. "Two hours?"

"When the sun sets," said Avram stoically.

"YOU'RE A MESH-A-GOONA!"

"*Meshuggene*," corrected Avram. He turned down the hill and pushed on.

By five forty-five in the afternoon, when they stopped again to rest on a low rise, the indistinct blotch that had been pursuing them resolved itself into five individual horsemen. (Of the original group, one had been shot, one had turned back, and one had gotten an attack of diarrhea and promised to catch up later.)

"They're comin'!" Tommy shouted.

Avram, desperately tired, began to run, Nuchshlepper padding along behind him. Tommy looked toward the horizon where the sun hung suspended, a deflating ocher sphere.

"Now?" he said.

Avram glanced up. "Not now," he gasped. He continued to run for another hundred yards, then slowed to a jog.

"Now?"

The sphere had become a crimson crescent.

"Almost," Avram gasped.

A mile away, the men in the posse were pointing and gesturing excitedly.

"Now?" asked Tommy, as the sky darkened.

Avram looked up. "Now," he said. He swung himself onto Nuchshlepper's back.

"Thank God," said Tommy, spurring his horse to a gallop.

● ● ●

(10)

Thousands of years ago, the Humboldt River, which crosses the state of Nevada, had a confluence with the Truckee, the Carson, and the Walker Rivers, all flowing down from the Sierra Nevada in California. The site of the intersection was a great lake, Lahontan, which stretched about one hundred seventy-five miles east-west and two hundred miles north-south, fed by rainfall from the mountains and vast amounts of melting snow. Gradually, however, the climate changed. As the weather became warmer and drier, Lahontan began to evaporate, leaving only Pyramid and Walker Lakes as bodies of water, turning the rest of the land into arid, barren desert.

179

By Saturday midnight, Avram and Tommy were five miles out in the Forty Mile Desert, which separates the last waters of the Humboldt from the first waters of either the Carson or the Truckee. Tommy had insisted that they push ahead through the night, not only to distance themselves from the posse but to avoid, as much as possible, the searing daylight heat.

Avram took a swallow of water from his canteen. "Bitter!" he said, making a face.

"All the water 'round here's bitter," said Tommy. "Some of it'll kill ya."

"It seems," said Avram, "that there's no end to this. That the hazards keep coming like plagues, and that eventually we will be caught up and succumb."

"Nah, we ain' gonna suck nothin'," said Tommy. "We almos' in California now. You jus' hang on, Cuz. You an' me's gonna make it."

"I admire your confidence," said Avram.

"You ain't the only one got faith," said Tommy. "Mine's jus' in a different place."

They slept fitfully from two to five in the morning, then started out again just before dawn. The sand was thick and heavy; by ten A.M. it was already blazing hot. The horses slowed down. Men and beasts became soaked with perspiration. Avram had long since removed his coat and hat. (His *yarmulka*, of course, stayed on.) The trail they took was lined with death: bleached skeletons of cows and oxen, human graves, abandoned furniture, broken wagons.

"Forty-niners," said Tommy. "Musta been a million of 'em come this way. Half of 'em didn'

180

know they ass from a six-shooter. Took more stuff than they could carry, had no directions, no guides, got cholera, got lost—ended up by the side of the trail there."

"A terrible pity," said Avram.

" 'Bout three years ago the Donner party came through here," said Tommy. "You ever heerd a them?"

Avram shook his head no.

"Real fucked-up bunch. Fightin' with each other, left one man right here in this desert. A old man, left him alone to die, like the Indians do. Rest of the party got caught in the Sierras in the winter an' starved. Et dogs, harnesses, shoes, everythin' they could find, finally et each other." He shrugged. "Some of 'em made it."

Avram, sickened, turned away.

They rested for an hour, then continued on. There was no shelter of any kind, no change in the terrain to relieve the monotony of the endless expanse of sand. Their water ran out before nightfall. Exhausted, they slept for eight hours, though they knew they should be traveling to take advantage of the night time coolness. "No use savin' time if you're dead when you get there," Tommy had said.

They resumed their journey at dawn. Avram, after his prayers, looked toward the east. "I don't see them," he said.

"Maybe your prayers been answered," Tommy suggested.

"I don't think God works so directly," said Avram, "except maybe in emergencies."

"What you call this?" said Tommy.

By the afternoon, their feet were covered with blisters, their lips were cracked and bleeding, and Avram had an upset stomach.

"The water from the Humboldt," said Tommy. "Does that to a lot of people."

"But I haven't had any since yesterday."

"Takes time to work."

They rested near a group of cacti. "In ancient Egypt," said Avram, bent over with pain, "the escaping Hebrew slaves were pursued by the Egyptians over the desert."

"Jus' like us," said Tommy.

"They didn't have time—the Hebrews—to leaven their bread, to add the yeast that would make it rise, so they ate unleavened cakes. Oy, my stomach is killing me."

"They baked these things in the sun?" asked Tommy, his mouth parched and lips chapped.

Avram shook his head. "We can't do it," he grunted. "You need water to mix with the flour."

Tommy shrugged. He walked to the nearest cactus, slit open one of the fleshy stems, then inverted it over his face. Avram looked on expectantly. Nothing happened.

"Well I ain't right *all* the time," said Tommy. "A man's got limits, ya know."

"I know," said Avram softly. "I know."

Their third day on the desert a dust storm blew up, driving the alkali sand hard against their faces, making it difficult to breathe. Their exposed skin began to burn and their eyes watered uncontrollably. With the wind came the stench of rotting animals. Avram could not decide which hurt more, the pain in his stomach, his eyes, or his sandpaper throat. A toss-up, he decided finally. After a half hour, the storm abated.

"When does this thing end?" asked Avram hoarsely. In addition to everything else, he was badly sunburned.

"You mean the desert?" said Tommy. "'Bout another seven, eight miles be my guess." He grinned. "You should see it in summer."

"I'll come back for a look," said Avram through parched lips.

Two miles later they came to a small, hot spring, bubbling in the middle of the sand. They dismounted, and Tommy kneeled, touched his hand to the water, and gingerly tasted one finger. "Bitter." He shook his head. "Could be poison."

"Wouldn't there be dead animals around if that was the case?" asked Avram.

"Maybe," said Tommy. "Maybe not. Maybe it takes a while to work." He paused. "My opinion, we wait till we git to the Truckee. I *know* that water is fresh."

But while they spoke, Nuchshlepper had wandered over to the edge of the water-hole and was now drinking voraciously. Avram went to the animal and gently pulled him back.

"He seems a little wobbly," said Avram.

Tommy raised his eyebrows. "Usually, a horse knows what's good for him. He senses it."

"Not him," said Avram. "I doubt it. He's Jewish. I don't think he knows from such things." He squinted at a small cloud in the distance. "Uh-oh, I think our friends are after us."

183

Tommy, who was watching Avram's horse, did not look. "Will you quit that? They ain't comin'."

"How can you be sure?"

"Because it's been three days an' they're hundreds of miles from home an' this is desert country. Even a crazy person don't chase you out here."

"Well *something* is coming," said Avram.

"It's a *mirage*," said Tommy. "Your mind is shot from the heat. It's playin' tricks on you."

"The tricks are getting bigger quite fast," said Avram.

"I'm tellin' you they ain't comin'. Now jus' relax."

"There are seven of them," said Avram. "How many were there before?"

That made Tommy raise his head. "Them's Indians!" he yelled, as the horsemen approached at full gallop. "Whyn't you tell me?"

"You didn't ask," said Avram.

"Le's go!"

They mounted, wheeled their horses and took off. The Indians chased them for about ten minutes, then appeared to give up. As they slowed to a walk after their frantic flight, Tommy's horse began to snort and whinny. Nuchshlepper was foaming at the mouth. Tommy raised himself up in the saddle and saw . . . water.

"Eeeeeeeaaaaaahoooo!" he shouted. "We done it. Yaaahooo! It's the Truckee, Cuz. We made it! We made it!"

"It's a miracle," said Avram. Then, suddenly, Nuchshlepper collapsed under him. Avram barely could get his feet out of the stirrups before the horse rolled over on his side. Tommy dismounted quickly, examined Nuchshlepper's rigid flanks, and then his nose and mouth. The horse's eyes were tightly shut.

"He plumb up an' died," said Tommy.

Avram stood stunned. "Died? But . . . Died?"

Tommy nodded.

Avram began to cry. He covered his face with his hands.

"C'mon," said Tommy. "First thing, we git us some water."

He removed Avram's saddle bags and carried them on his shoulders, leading Avram the two hundred yards to the shallow banks of the Truckee. "Slow, now," he said. They drank, as did Tommy's horse. "You drink too much or too fast an' you like to bust. Easy . . . easy . . ."

When Avram had swallowed several mouthfuls, he stood up and trudged back toward the desert.

"Hey," said Tommy, "where you goin'?"

"I'll just be a few minutes," said Avram.

Tommy watched as Avram approached his dead horse, saw him scoop up handfuls of sand and cover the animal until it was completely obscured. Even hundreds of yards away, the chanting was clearly audible. And though it was in another language, the meaning was clear.

"*Yis-ga-dal v'yis-ka-dash she-may rabo. B'ol-mo dee-v'ro hir'-oosay v'yamleech . . .*"

Finally Avram stood up, lingered a final moment, then trudged back to Tommy. "*Kaddish,*" he said. "A prayer for the dead. It's the least a Jew should have."

Tommy nodded, and Avram returned to the river for another drink. "What did they want?" he said when his thirst was quenched and he had soaked his face and arms in the water.

"Who?"

"The Indians."

"Our horses, prob'ly," said Tommy. "Guns, maybe. Scalps, heads—Jesus, I don't know. They wanted our tukases, that's what they wanted."

"But why?"

They been shit on by white men so long they don't ask questions no more."

Avram nodded. "I guess I can understand their feelings."

"You might look on it different if they'd a got a little closer," said Tommy.

"What, uh, type of Indians were they exactly?" asked Avram.

"Hard to say at that distance," said Tommy. "Paiutes, mos' likely. Maybe Washo. Could even be Shoshone or Mojave."

"They decorate themselves very colorfully," said Avram.

Tommy shook his head. "They wasn't painted up fer one of your *Bar Mitzvahs,* I can tell you that."

Avram's gaze wandered over to his saddle bags, now resting on the ground. In the heat of the escape and in his pain and thirst, he had not taken time to check his possessions.

"Oh, my God!" he said.

"What?"

"The Torah!!"

"What happened?"

"It's missing." Avram began to moan. "Oh God, it's missing, it's missing." He clenched his fist. "I had it in that yellow poncho . . ." He began to sway from side to side.

"It was danglin' from your saddle horn, right?"

"Yes, yes," said Avram. "God, it must've somehow slipped out!" He headed back into the desert.

"Wait!" shouted Tommy.

Avram did not slow down.

"Wait, goddammit! I ain't goin' with you this time!" called Tommy.

Avram seemed not to hear.

Tommy caught up to him and grabbed his arm. "Did you unnerstan' me?"

Avram removed Tommy's hand from his arm and continued forward. "I did."

"That was war paint those Injuns wore, you dumb ignoramus."

No response.

"They won't talk—they'll jus' kill you!"

The distance between them increased as Tommy stopped walking.

"I ain't goin', you sonofabitch!"

Avram looked back, but kept moving. "Who asked you to?"

"So long, sucker!"

Avram trudged ahead.

"Have a nice funeral!"

After five minutes, the rabbi was a tiny, far-off figure, weaving uncertainly through the sand.

Tommy returned to his horse. "You dumb asshole!" he shouted defiantly at the desert.

● ● ●

An hour later, surrounded by Indian braves, Tommy and Avram were marched into a village of small, rounded huts.

"Jus' tell me what come over me," said Tommy.

"You don't recognize it yet?" said Avram. Nervously, he checked the brave nearest him, who rode with the Torah slung over his saddle.

"I think I los' mah sense," said Tommy. "Tha's the only logical explanation fer why I keep savin' your ass."

"This time, you haven't saved it," said Avram. Clusters of old and young women, children, and skinny dogs watched him curiously as he walked. Several of the women were weaving baskets made of reeds.

"This time you gonna die, an' me with ya, because tha's what happens when you act like a asshole."

"Me?" said Avram.

"Me."

"You acted like what you are," said Avram. "A friend. I would do the same for you."

"Would ya?"

"Yes."

"Well, next time I'm in Gal-whatever—"

"Galicia."

"Yeah. Next time I'm over there I might jus' check that out."

"I'd welcome the opportunity," said Avram.

The braves stopped them in an open space amid the huts. Avram studied the structures, each a frame of poles erected in a circle and connected at the top, then covered with layers of brush, reeds, and mud. Two muscular braves, dressed in antelope hides, stepped forward into the clearing.

"Jus' keep your mouth shut," said Tommy.

"Fine," said Avram.

"Let me do the talkin'."

"You know their language?"

"Not exactly. But all Indians talk with signs. You watch."

Avram nodded. Except for the two braves who'd come to meet them, he noticed most of the people in the camp were nearly naked. Many of the women had tattoos on their chins and caked red mud on their faces. He looked on, fascinated, as Tommy made elaborate hand and elbow movements.

"We come in peace," said Tommy, translating as he gestured.

The braves remained impassive.

"We don' want your land!"

The braves looked at each other.

"We don' want your buffalo!"

One of the braves folded his arms.

"We don' want your horses."

Stony silence.

"We don' want your women."

The Indians studied Tommy intently.

"We don' want nothin! TRUST ME!"

The brave with folded arms nodded solemnly, at which point the other brave swung a war club that hit Tommy directly in the jaw, knocking him unconscious. From somewhere a drum beat started up. Avram was suddenly seized and dragged toward one of four poles that had been set into the ground. A number of children spit at him.

"Hey!" said Avram to a bare-breasted woman nearby whom he took to be their mother. "You should teach them some manners."

The woman spit at him also.

Four men tied his hands behind him and bound him to a stake. The still-unconscious Tommy was trussed similarly alongside him. Several of the men prodded Avram's body with sharpened sticks.

"Hey! Don't do that! Hey, mister, please . . ."

Tommy began to moan. A small boy, perhaps three or four years old, came up to Avram and smiled.

"Hello," said Avram, the terror beginning to build as men began to pile brush and twigs in front of him. "You look like a nice little fellow. What's your name?" A show of friendliness, he hoped, would demonstrate to the Indians his basic good nature.

The boy burst into tears and began to scream.

"Oh, Christ," mumbled Tommy.

"I think you should try reasoning with them," said Avram.

Tommy shook himself fully awake. "How?" he said. "My hands are tied, I can't even make sign language."

"Oy," said Avram.

Tommy looked around as the brush and twigs rose past his waist. "Oh, God," he wailed. "Not like this. I don' wanna die. Please."

Avram, greatly unnerved by this display

from his usually confident friend, asked, "What are they doing? What's going to happen?"

"They gonna roast us. Gonna burn us alive."

"Oy, oy," said Avram. "Oy, *Gottenyu!* God forbid." He saw an old man emerge from one of the huts, accompanied by a young brave. In the brave's hand was a lit torch. Avram began to chant in Hebrew from the Book of Psalms.

"Be pleased, O Lord, to deliver me! O Lord, make haste to help me! Let them be put to shame and confusion altogether who seek to snatch away my life. Let them be turned back and brought to dishonor who desire my hurt! Let them be appalled because of their shame, who say to me, 'Aha, Aha!' "

The old man and the torch bearer paused in front of Avram's stake.

"Oh, no . . ." said Tommy. He turned his face away. "Oh no. How'd I git inta this? He looked back at Avram. "Aw, Jeee-sus."

The brave with the torch knelt down, the flames inches away from the kindling. Avram, perspiring, had closed his eyes. In a low voice he continued to chant Psalm 40, as the old man watched him curiously.

"Who the hell are you?" said the Indian finally.

Avram's eyes snapped open. "Who the—me . . . me rabbi!" he said excitedly. "Jewish rabbi."

"I have heard your tongue before," said the man.

"Come from far away," babbled Avram. "Across big ocean. I read much books on Indians."

"You don't speak English very well," said

191

the man. He whispered something to a nearby brave, who ran to one of the huts.

"He's the chief," whispered Tommy to Avram. He cleared his throat and addressed himself to the old man. "He's a very holy person, Chief. He talks to the spirits every mornin' an' every night."

"Ah," said the chief. "A medicine man."

"That's it!" said Tommy. "You got it. Very similar, very similar."

"Can he cure baldness?" asked the chief.

"Can he cure, uh—" Tommy gulped, turned toward Avram. "Can you?"

Avram shook his head.

"Once," said the chief, "we had a *khathali* who claimed he could restore hair. His cure was to shoot the bald man in the Adam's apple with something taken from the head of an otter." He paused. "He was very crazy."

"Well, this man ain't at all crazy," said Tommy, motioning with his chin toward Avram. "He's kind and good and gentle, a reg'lar sweetheart."

"He sounds like a woman," said the chief.

"Oh, no. No, not at all. Hell, he helped rob a bank an' got chased by a posse—no sir, he ain't no woman, not by a long shot. An' what's more, all that time, even with men after us, he wouldn't ride on a Saturday. No siree!"

"I have heard of this sacred day," said the chief.

"That's right," said Tommy, "that's his holy—You heerd of it?"

"Oh yes," said the chief. "I have met many white men. A few were like him."

Tommy grinned nervously. "Well, then you knows what fine folks they is. How they don't like to anger the spirits. How they loves the Indians—and so do I—and don't mean no harm to nobody."

The chief considered. "Can he make rain?"

"Rain? Jesus H. Christ, you shoulda seed the rain this man made. I mean buckets of rain, pourin'—"

"What are you telling him?" said Avram.

Tommy shot him a frantic glance. "—pourin' down, day after day."

"Even on the desert?" asked the chief.

"Anywhere. Anyplace, anytime. I didn't know what the hell we was gonna do with it all. An' if you wanna talk about snow . . ."

The chief raised his hand for Tommy to be silent. "Don't talk about snow."

"Okay, okay," said Tommy quickly. "It's your show, Chief."

The chief turned to Avram. "You are our guests here."

Avram looked at him in wonder. "Your guests? But then . . . why are we tied? Why are you getting ready to burn us?"

The chief wrinkled his brow. "I am amazed at your stupidity," he said.

"Forgive me," said Avram, "but I do not . . ." His voice trailed off.

"How else," said the chief, his voice raised in annoyance, "are we to honor our guests and permit them to show themselves worthy of divine protection . . . than by submitting them to torture?"

"Well," said Avram, "maybe I could suggest . . ."

The chief again held up his hand for silence. "Perhaps you would prefer a different ordeal," he said. "I have traveled among many tribes, I have seen many different honors. Our Plains brothers, for instance, run skewers through the fleshy parts of the back and then tie thongs between them and the Sun-pole. After the honoree is drawn up off the ground, he throws his weight against the skewers until they are torn out." He paused. "Would this ceremony please you more?"

Avram closed his eyes. "Uh, it's not exactly what I had in mind, Chief. I don't think—"

"Here's one of my personal favorites," interrupted the old man. "The guest removes his clothes and his body is smeared all over with ceremonial honey, particularly on the genitalia. Then, naked, he is tied down upon an anthill, and his flesh is consumed by the myriads of tiny, scurrying insects." The chief chuckled as he completed the description, and his eyes twinkled. "If you like, this could be arranged, although our supply of honey is limited. We do have plenty of ants, though."

"I believe I'll pass," said Avram. He saw Tommy relax slightly in his bonds.

"Certain other people," continued the chief, "have ordeals in which the honored guests are given a mixture of herbs and the 'black drink,' . . . . and are then flogged and sent out into the desert. There, for seven days and seven nights, they spew vomit and feces, and this purgation leaves mind and body free for the receipt of new impressions."

194

"That's it!" shouted Tommy. "I'll take that one, Chief. Give me the shits an' heaves anytime over burnin'. I'll take that one."

"That one is disgusting," said the chief solemnly. "We do not use that one."

The brave who had earlier been sent to one of the huts reappeared now, carrying Avram's yellow poncho. He handed it to the chief, the Torah scrolls peeking out from the loose covering.

"You come for this?" asked the chief.

"Yes."

"I have read this book."

Avram stared at him in amazement.

"I did not understand one word."

"I didn't git it either," offered Tommy. "But he kin explain it to—" He stopped when the chief looked at him sharply.

"What do you call this book?" asked the old man.

"Torah," said Avram hoarsely.

"Would you trade your horse for Torah?"

"My horse died," said Avram.

"But would you trade your horse if you had one?"

"Yes."

"Your horse and your boots?"

"Yes."

"And your clothes?"

"Yes."

"And everything else that you own?"

"Yes."

The chief paused. "Even your knife?"

"I don't have a knife."

The chief looked incredulous. "You have no knife?"

"No."

The chief shook his head. "No knife and no horse. You are a poor man indeed."

"Poverty is not measured by a man's material possessions," said Avram. "True poverty is only in the spirit."

"Your words are courageous," said the chief. "If I give you back this Torah—will you purify your soul through fire?"

Avram saw the veins stand out on Tommy's neck. An angry welt had risen on the point of his jaw, where the brave had clubbed him.

Avram inhaled. "Yes," he said simply.

"Awwwwww sheeeeeeee," said Tommy.

The chief nodded to the brave with the torch, who had remained kneeling beside him. The warrior dipped the torch twice, and the piles of kindling that surrounded each of the strange white intruders burst into crackling flames.

(11)

The fires rose quickly until the flames were up near the men's faces. Tommy began to cough from the smoke. Sweat poured down Avram's forehead.

"If I let you go," said the chief to Avram, "may I keep the Torah?"

"No," said Avram firmly.

The pain from the intense heat was almost unbearable. He heard Tommy begin a low moan, a moan that rose rapidly to become a scream.

"Are you certain?" asked the chief.

The flames licked cruelly at the fleshy parts of Avram's legs and arms. He shrieked in agony. The skin on several fingers began to blacken. A raging wall of incandescent orange shimmered and danced before his eyes. I come to you, God, thought Avram. Now I come. With his last strength, he screamed. "Yes, I'm certain!"

And then, abruptly, the orange wall had a gaping hole in it; seconds later it had crumbled entirely. Braves were shoving the kindling off to one side, others smothered the fire with antelope hides. Avram saw that the chief was smiling.

"Rabbi with no knife—you are a brave man. Brave not only in word but in action."

"Thank you," whispered Avram.

"And you"—the chief turned to Tommy—"who speaks to Indians as if to little children—your heart is big."

Tommy nodded and forced a faint smile.

"Not as big as your mouth," said the chief, "but you have good feelings inside."

"Thank you, Chief," said Tommy. "Thank you very much."

At a signal from the old man, two braves cut the thongs that bound Tommy's and Avram's hands.

"Now," said the chief, "we go into my wiki-up and we talk."

Tommy and Avram followed the old man to a nearby hut, much larger than the others, and found a number of people already seated on the ground inside. "We have seen Jews before," declared the chief, motioning for them to recline next to him.

"You have?" said Avram.

"Oh yes. About six or seven moons ago. They, too, had the curly lines of hair on their faces and spoke poor English."

"Were they on their way to California?" asked Avram.

"Yes, they were," said the chief, "but we burned them and so they did not get there."

Avram stiffened.

"They said they came from a place called—" The chief stopped and looked at the medicine man on his right.

"Germany," said the medicine man.

"The woman was most hateful," said the chief. "She called us savages. The man told us we were an inferior race. Nevertheless, we gave them the opportunity to restore their honor by an ordeal, but they died badly. The children, we sold to the Bannock, but first we took their names."

Avram looked blank.

"So they would be nameless in the spirit world," explained the medicine man, "and not be able to call each other to band against us."

"I will explain," said the chief. "My Moquat Paiute name is Natimucca, but my Jewish name is Solomon Cohen." He indicated a dark-skinned woman next to Avram. "This is my wife, Linda Cohen."

Avram smiled politely, but the woman did not respond.

"And my children," continued Natimucca, indicating three straight-haired youngsters. "Michael, Debra, and Jeffrey Cohen."

Avram nodded. "I think that Indians and Jews have much in common," he said.

"This is so," said Natimucca. "I have noticed that Jews also have large noses."

"I meant about being oppressed," said Avram.

Natimucca seemed puzzled. He turned to

the medicine man, who looked equally per-plexed. "Oppressed?" said the chief. "What is 'oppressed'?"

"Well," said Avram, "for instance, the white men steal your buffalo."

"What's a buffalo?" said the medicine man.

Natimucca smiled. "Pawanat is not sophis-ticated. He has not been around like me. I have been all over, seen everything white and Indian." He turned to the medicine man. "A buffalo is like a giant, lumpy cow, only bigger."

"Not like an antelope?" said Pawanat.

"No, nothing at all." He returned his atten-tion to Tommy and Avram. "Oh yes, I am most familiar with the white man's ways. I have lis-tened to the whispering spirit, and—"

"I'm sorry," interrupted Avram.

"The wire that sings."

"The telegraph," interpreted Tommy.

"Yes," said Natimucca. "And I have ridden the iron wagon that coughs smoke. And worn the white man's tall hats. And fired the white man's long guns."

"You're a man of culture, Chief," said Tommy.

"Culture, yes," said Natimucca. "The white man has brought us many things. He has given us the sex disease that makes urination so pain-ful, and the illness you call small pox that kills entire villages. He has given us alcohol that destroys the mind and guns that explode in our hands. But worst of all, worst of all, he has given us the disease of sadness that makes strong young braves sulk in their wikiups and toss sleeplessly at night and have no appetite for food."

Avram was amazed. "You mean . . . you mean depression?" A woman leaned over him and rubbed some salve on his scorched fingers. Immediately, the burning ceased. Outside, the sun was sinking below the horizon.

"We can see our destiny," said Natimucca simply. "And there is no hope."

"Ah, I disagree," said Avram. "There is always hope."

The chief motioned to a brave to bring over two shallow bowls. He handed one each to Avram and Tommy. "Excuse me," he said, "I have been a poor host. Here, eat and enjoy."

Avram looked into the bowl and immediately suppressed a retch. Natimucca noticed however.

"You do not like roasted grasshoppers?" he asked.

"Well . . ." said Avram. "It's just . . . Jews have certain dietary laws. . . ."

"Ah, yes. I have heard of these. Perhaps you'd prefer beetle cakes or crushed worms."

"I'm sorry," said Avram. "The rules of *kashrut* do not permit." Actually, certain locusts were in fact allowed, but there was no way of telling if the ones before him were the right kind.

"Even animals are forbidden?"

"Certain ones. But all must be slaughtered in a special way."

"Perhaps a rabbit," said the chief. "We make a net from sagebrush and tule rushes, a net as high as a man's shoulder and as long as ten horses. Then we place this net across a narrow space in the rocks and drive the rabbits into it. When they are trapped, we club them to death."

"I'm sorry," said Avram. "Rabbits are forbidden. Animals must have cloven hoofs and their stomachs must have four compartments."

Natimucca's face brightened. "Like an antelope!"

"Yes," said Avram slowly. "I believe an antelope is an approved mammal."

The chief's face quickly dropped. "We don't have any antelope." He paused and looked at Tommy. "But you . . . you can eat, yes?"

Tommy stared glumly at the grasshoppers.

"Enjoy!" said the chief expectantly.

Reluctantly, Tommy chomped off a part of one insect and forced himself to swallow it. "Good," he said unenthusiastically.

Natimucca shrugged. "Not good," he said, "but at least you don't starve." He turned back to Avram. "Jews must starve," he said.

"Some of them," said Avram.

"No wonder," said Natimucca. "There is hardly anything you can eat." He paused. "How about piñon nuts? Are these allowed?"

"All fruits and vegetables are permitted," said Avram.

Again, Natimucca's face brightened. He motioned to his wife who brought over a plate of brownish nuts. Avram tasted one. "Very good," he said, "really very good."

"Your god is a harsh god," said Pawanat, "to forbid you so much food."

"Perhaps," said Avram. "But he gives us many things in return for our sacrifices."

"Can your god make rain?" asked Natimucca.

"Yes," said Avram.

"But he doesn't."

"That's right."

"Why?"

"Because that's not his department."

"But if he wanted to, he could?"

"Yes."

"What kind of a god do you have?"

"Don't say *my* god," said Avram. "He is God. He is your God as well."

"Don't give him to us," said Natimucca.

"But why—"

"Because we have enough troubles with our own gods. We live in fear of them. They are in the desert and the yucca plants, in the lakes and in the mountains. Always, always they want sacrifices and presents, and very seldom do they help us."

"We believe there is only one God," said Avram.

"Only one?" said Natimucca. "He must be very lonesome. What does he do?"

"He can do anything," said Avram.

"Then why can't he make rain?" asked Pawanat.

"Because He doesn't choose to," said Avram.

"Then being alone has made him cruel," speculated Natimucca.

"On the contrary," said Avram, touching the Torah, which the chief had placed beside him. "He gives us strength when we are suffering. He gives us compassion when we feel hatred. He gives us hope when we feel only despair. He gives us courage when we search about blindly in the darkness."

"But he does not make rain."

Avram shook his head sadly. "No. He does not make—"

Outside, a giant flash of jagged lightning streaked across the evening sky. The light came through the open top of the wickiup, bathing the interior in a flickering, ghostly blue. There was a huge rumble of thunder; then, seconds later, thousands of droplets tattooed the roof of the hut and came down the unprotected center.

"Of course," said Avram, "sometimes . . . just like that"—he snapped his fingers ineptly—"He'll change His mind."

There was a loud murmuring from the assembled braves. Some of them began to chant. Pawanat stood up, muttered something to Natimucca, bowed once to Avram, and left the wickiup.

"He says your God is very impressive," said Natimucca. "Our own gods have been unable to produce rain for many moons. Pawanat has gone to question them."

Avram nodded sheepishly.

Natimucca rose, as did the others in the hut. "And now, you rest," he said. "You are tired from your ordeal. Later, we talk again."

The Indians filed out of the hut.

Tommy stared at Avram. "That rain," he said. "That really weren't no doin' a yourn." He hesitated. "Were it?"

Avram grinned.

● ● ●

Later in the evening, after Tommy and Avram had slept for several hours, the Indians, including Pawanat, returned to the hut. A low fire was started in the center and smoke curled up through the roof.

"I have been thinking," said Natimucca to Avram, "about your idea that Jews and Indians are alike. And I remember once, long ago, a traveler here—one of those you call Mormons—told us that we are descended from tribes of Jews who were banished long ago from far-away lands."

"The Lost Tribes . . ." murmured Avram.

"You know of this?"

"It is speculation," said Avram. "Legend. There is an account in the Bible of Ten Tribes of the Kingdom of Israel which the king of Assyria carried away and placed in Halah, and in Habor, on the river Gozan, and in the cities of the Medes. They were to stay in these places until a Messiah came to lead them back to Zion. But it's just a legend. No one has ever traced them."

"But it might be true?"

"It might. . . ."

"Then until it is proven wrong," said Natimucca, "I will think of you as my brother." At this, he stood up and removed a sheath from his waist. Inside it was a knife. He handed it to Avram. "I wish that you would accept this gift, that you may think of me with good memories in your old age."

Avram hesitated.

"It would make me very happy," continued Natimucca.

Avram took the knife, admiring the detailed carvings on its handle, and strapped it to his body. "Thank you," he said. "I accept with gratitude."

"Now," said Natimucca, "I will no longer have to worry that my Jewish friend has no knife."

Pawanat approached Avram with a bowl. More grasshoppers, thought Avram. But when he looked, he saw only a bunch of what appeared to be sliced chestnuts, except that they were covered with tufts of white down.

"We wonder if you would honor us," said Pawanat, "by taking part in our prayer ceremony. We pray particularly for one of our tribe who has the white man's coughing sickness."

"Certainly, I will pray," said Avram.

Pawanat gave him four of the "nuts" and moved on to Tommy. "And you?"

"Sure," said Tommy. "Why not?"

Each man in the hut was given his allotment from the bowl. The women, however, were ignored, and they clustered near the periphery, away from the fire. Pawanat began a guttural chant, to the accompaniment of a drum and rattle. At a signal, the men began eating.

"Watch out for this stuff," whispered Tommy to Avram.

"Why?" whispered back Avram. "Vegetables are okay."

"These ain' jus' vegetables. These is peyote buttons."

"Never heard of it."

"Jus' watch out."

"Eat!" said Natimucca.

Avram peeled the fuzz off the top of one button, then took a bite. "Good," he said.

Natimucca nodded. The ceremony lasted until dawn, each man in the hut singing four songs in turn (Avram chanted various psalms; Tommy got halfway through a low-key "Sweet Betsy From Pike" before claiming a sore throat), and being given various additional allotments of peyote. The lullaby of the chants, the rhythmical drumming and rattling, the glare of the fire—all combined to produce a strangely relaxed and hypnotic effect. The fact that by first daylight, when the Morning Star song was sung, Avram had consumed twenty-four peyote buttons did not hurt either. At the ceremony's end, burnt lizards were passed around for everyone's enjoyment (Tommy and Avram were thoughtfully given more peyote buttons instead), and the Meat song was sung in gratitude.

"So," said Natimucca to Avram, who had passed out and reawakened several times during the night, "you have seen our prayer ritual."

"Very fine," said Avram.

"Now we can enjoy ourselves," said Natimucca. "What do Jewish people do for amusement?"

"Same as Indians," said Avram. "They dance."

Natimucca rose. "Show me," he said.

They stepped outside, where most of the villagers had gathered near the chief's hut.

"I'm not a very good dancer," said Avram, chewing his last button.

"Do you feel joy?" said Natimucca. New drumming had begun.

"Very much," said Avram, his head buzzing. "Yes."

"Then show me, please. Dance with my people."

The chief addressed himself to a line of braves waiting nearby. "I want him to dance with you. He will teach and you will learn."

One of the braves motioned to Avram, who tentatively stepped forward, putting an arm around the waist to his left and another around the waist to his right. The drumming became louder and the assembled villagers began to chant. The men in the line began to move in a circle, their footwork uncertain, as they watched Avram try to imitate their steps instead of initiating his own. As the chanting subsided, however, Avram gradually took the initiative.

"*Havah nagila, havah nagila, havah nagila, vehnismacha. Havah naroninah, havah . . .*" His voice rang out through the clear morning air and was joined after a while by those of the tribesmen. The circle of braves moved around faster and faster, kicking, whirling, the dance metamorphosing finally into a full fledged hora.

"*. . . Ooroo, ooroo achim, ooroo achim balev samayach, ooroo achim balev samayach . . .*"

Faces spun past Avram—Tommy, Natimucca, Pawanat, a bevy of toothless women, the child who'd first smiled at him, drummers, rattlers, naked braves . . . Bodies began to blend, to grow indistinct, the drumming seemed to come from inside his own head, the huts and ground and people all beginning to liquefy, to melt, the earth corkscrewing, spiraling upward in a dizzy, hurtling rush. . . .

Blackness.

• • •

His back hurt. Slowly, Avram forced open his eyes. "That was some dan—"

He stopped.

He was lying on a bed made of boards in a small, stone cell. Except for a crude wooden chair and tiny table, the room seemed entirely bare. Not quite—on one wall, a tapestry hung, a large red crucifix embroidered on a brown background. Shafts of sunlight filtered in through a barred window.

Avram was conscious of a weight on him. He reached out, felt the twin scrolls of his Torah unwrapped across his chest. He rolled his eyes sideways and saw a bald man with a circular fringe of hair gazing at him curiously.

"Hello," said Avram.

The man nodded.

"Where am I?" asked Avram.

The man smiled sweetly.

"I hear bells," said Avram.

The man nodded again.

An idea began to dawn on Avram, a possibility . . . "Oy veh, I'm not, uh . . . This isn't . . . Listen, am I . . ."

The man shook his head—no.

Avram exhaled in relief. "I was a little sick, I think."

The man nodded yes.

"Do you want to ask me anything?" said Avram.

A voice came from the doorway. "He can't, Cuz."

Avram sat up.

209

At the entrance, Tommy stood hands on hips, grinning. "I'll explain it to ya later. These guys is all monks. Their religion don' let 'em say shit." He waved briskly to the monk in the room, who smiled back. "C'mon, supper's waitin'."

Avram stood up, wobbled, regained his balance. "But where are we? What day is it? How long have we been here?"

Tommy came over to steady him. "Jus' take it slow, an' le's get some grub. You oughta be pretty hungry by now—you been outa yer head fer almos' three days."

Avram clutched the Torah tightly in his hands.

"You really had me worried, you know that?" said Tommy. "Leave that Torah here. I had enough trouble with that thing, Mr. No-Knife. It'll be perfectly safe with Brother Andrew."

The monk bowed, a grave expression on his face. Avram laid the Torah next to the wooden bed, bowed in return, then was half-pushed, half-carried out the door by Tommy. They walked through a covered arcade lined with massive, adobe-block pillars beyond which was a quadrangular courtyard.

"These things melt in the rain," said Tommy, indicating the pillars. "They stucco 'em with lime but it don' help much." He looked back at Avram. "Jesus, you really had me worried."

"What is this place?"

"This here is a mission," said Tommy. "San Scholastica de Nursia is what they calls it. 'Bout two miles west of Sonora."

"California?"

"Yeah, California. You missed the entire

trip. Natimucca had six braves take us all the way. Good thing, too. You made the whole trek slung over one of the horses."

Avram shook his head in amazement. "I remember nothing. . . ."

"Oh, yeah," said Tommy. "Came right through Walker Pass. Now you kin tell everyone how you seed the Sierra Nevada, an' how wonderful they was."

"I was out the whole time, huh?"

"Oh, you woke once or twice," said Tommy. "Babbled somethin', then went back to sleep. Don't think a herd a buffalo woulda woke ya."

As they turned a corner, Avram saw across the patio a scalloped wall with bells suspended in the apertures.

"Spanish," said Tommy. "They call it a *companario*."

"It's very pretty," said Avram.

Tommy shook his head. "Damn!" he said. "Didn' I tell ya to watch out fer that peyote?"

"Please," said Avram, "don't be so upset."

"Upset? Who's upset? I ain' upset. But why don'tcha listen to me when I tell ya somethin'? You think I'm talkin' fer my health?"

"I apologize," said Avram.

"If I tell ya somethin', it's fer yer own damn good. What's the point of all my 'xperience?"

They paused outside a heavy wooden door set into a stone wall. Inside, Avram could hear movements, but no voices.

"That Brother Andrew," said Avram. "Was he a mute?"

"They all mute," said Tommy.

"You mean they never say anything?"

211

"They's called Trappists," said Tommy. "Though I ain't seed 'em trap nothin', leastways no beaver. Heerd about 'em from the Indians. Once they takes the vow, they stop talkin'."

"Completely?"

"I mean not a word." Tommy indicated an elderly monk approaching. "See that old man there? That's Father Joseph. Ain't spoke in twenty-five years."

Avram tried to absorb the immensity of this. "Twenty-five . . ."

"Not one word!"

"I've read about these things in Galicia. But, you know, it's like America—I knew it was there, although I never believed it until I saw with my own eyes." Avram shook his head. "Twenty-five years . . ."

They passed through the heavy door into a large dining room, as spare as the cell in which Avram had awakened. About twenty monks sat at a long wooden table. Avram and Tommy took chairs facing a huge crucifix mounted on one of the stone walls. The elderly monk seated himself at the front of the room. A moment later all the men bowed their heads in prayer, and then Indian servants began setting out plates and silverware and bowls of food.

Avram helped himself to some bread and corn cakes. "How come you know so much about this place if nobody here talks?" he whispered to Tommy.

"Oh, some talk," said Tommy quietly. "Indians. A lot of 'em live in the mission, includin' some from Natimucca's tribe."

"They live here? But why?"

212

Tommy stuffed a juicy piece of meat in his mouth. "Well, the padres teaches 'em stuff, fer one thing. Teach 'em tannin', an' blacksmithin' an' how to work crops, that type activity. That's what they's here for, to civilize the savages an' explain 'em all about Christ."

"And the Indians are interested in this?" asked Avram.

"They don' care shit about it," said Tommy. "Only reason they here is 'cause the padres give 'em three squares a day, an' if you seed what them Paiutes ate, you know the difference. Only trouble is, th' Indians gotta do work in return, till the fields or make them adobe blocks, an' there's a corporal's guard—maybe ten men or so— that keeps 'em from leavin' the compound. They hunt down runaways and brings 'em back."

"But that's terrible," said Avram. "Why would anyone want to stay here?"

Tommy belched and bit down on a piece of chicken. "Like I said, a full belly is a powerful argument. Besides, th' Indians is allowed to visit they own village one week outa every five. It could be worse."

Avram smiled sadly. Tommy's last words, of course, were the motto of Avram's father. Avram thought about his parents back in Galicia, whom he would never see again, about Rebbe Gittelman. Had word somehow gotten to them from San Francisco that Avram hadn't made it? Did they believe him dead? Were they mourning him? Had Mendl Pincus, eighty-eighth in the *yeshiva* class, finally moved up to eighty-seventh? Avram tried to banish the subject from his mind. He reached out for some grapes, tasted them, and found them exceptionally sweet and juicy. "Good!" he said.

The monk next to him smiled.

"Tha's Brother Bruno," said Tommy.

"I like this food, Brother Bruno," said Avram. "I know not to ask you any questions."

Brother Bruno nodded appreciatively.

"Don't worry—I understand. You know, all your vegetables are delicious. Do you grow them here or do you tr— Oh! Sorry. Sorry, I understand. No talking."

Brother Bruno held a finger to his lips.

"Believe me," said Avram, "your message has been received. I understand. It's just that I'm not used to it, you know."

Brother Bruno nodded cheerfully.

Avram took another piece of bread. "Say," he called, "could someone pass the salt, please? The salt."

A small plate of salt was handed down the table. Brother Bruno placed it in front of Avram. "Thanks!" said Avram.

"You're welcome," said Brother Bruno. Immediately, he began to choke and turn red. He clasped a hand to his mouth, as if trying to force the words back inside. The other monks were staring at him intently.

Avram, cringing in embarrassment, tried to yammer apologies, but he could only stutter. "I . . . I . . . I'm so, so . . . I—"

"Shee-it," whispered Tommy.

And then, at the head of the table, Father Joseph, who had not uttered a sound in twenty-five years, began to laugh. Taking a cue, the other monks joined in. Sheepish sniggers became

214

open chuckles that gradually escalated to loud guffaws that went on quickly to flat-out hysteria. Brother Bruno, who had been choking with shame, now choked with mirth. Avram was giggling uncontrollably. Tommy was slapping his thighs and crumbling helplessly in his chair.

Father Joseph rapped sharply on the table with his knuckles. The laughter stopped abruptly; the monks returned to eating in silence. Avram lowered his head and tried to think solemn thoughts.

(12)

They departed at dawn the next day. The Paiutes had left a horse for Avram (Tommy said it was a gift, failing to mention that he'd given the Indians fifteen dollars in payment), and they rode out, past the mission cemetery and the small, separate buildings used for pottery and weaving. In a nearby field a group of Indians were chanting in Spanish.

"*Alabado*," said Tommy. "Mornin' hymn. 'Course, they got the tune all screwed up 'cause the monks here can't teach 'em."

"It's sad," said Avram reflectively. "I think they mean well, but I wonder if ultimately they're really benefiting those Indians."

"Shit if I know," said Tommy.

They headed west and south, following the

Stanislaus River, camping near Modesto, then continuing on through the San Joaquin Valley to San Jose. They arrived near dusk and let their horses amble down the main street. San Jose was a sleepy Spanish town that had been transformed by the gold rush. A supply base for prospectors, its permanent population was about three thousand, but transients easily numbered five times that. Red tiled, white-washed buildings alternated with two-story, wood-front hotels, plank hovels, brick assay offices, and occasional log cabins. Mexicans in black hats and heavy boots mingled with eastern business men, southern trappers, bearded miners, Indian laborers and Chinese brothel masters. Spanish women in lace *mantillas* and shawls bumped shoulders with prostitutes from France and kidnapped waifs from the Marquesas Islands. Huge red and blue signs on canvas façades advertised liquors of every sort, pork, flour, beans, pickles, soap, Boston crackers, mattresses, blankets, miners' heavy velvet coats and pantaloons, flannel shirts and drawers, Guernsey frocks, rubber waders, cradles, shovels, spades, axes, medicines for dysentery, ague and scurvy, newspapers from the East, books, and insurance on parcels of gold dust.

"I don't see what I'm looking for," said Avram.

"Then it don't exist," said Tommy.

"It exists," said Avram. He called to a miner walking across the street. "Excuse me . . ."

The man looked up.

"I was just wondering," said Avram, "is there a mail service in this town?"

"Down the street," said the man, "just past

Murderer's Bar an' before Cut Eye's Bar. Abe Beatty's Hotel an' Stables, it's called. Transfer point fer Concord Coach."

"Thank you," said Avram.

"Part of Overland Mail," called the man. "Stage leaves twice a week."

A moment later, Avram was dismounting in front of a wood, two-story building.

"You ain't gonna do what I think you're gonna do," said Tommy.

"I am," said Avram.

"I don' believe it. No one is that stupid."

"I am," repeated Avram.

He disappeared inside the building. Ten minutes later he was back out. Tommy was leaning against the hitching rail. "You *did* do what I thought you would?" he asked.

"Yes," said Avram placidly.

"You up an' returned the money?"

"Yes."

"But . . . but . . . that ain't the American way," Tommy sputtered. "That's . . . damn . . . that's crazy."

Avram shrugged.

"What's more, you ain't got no money left."

"That's right."

"So what're ya gonna do about it?"

"I don't know."

"You don't know," said Tommy derisively. "You don't know."

"No."

"Well, I'll tell you what I'm gonna do. I'm gonna git me a bath, an' then I'm gonna git drunk, an' catch me a whore with great big tits, then I'm gonna git drunk again, an' then . . ."

219

"You're out of ideas, maybe?" said Avram.

"No, I ain' outa ideas! Then I'm gonna rob this here Overland Mail office an' git my money back, you dumb-ass Jew!" Tommy headed across the street to the Empire Hotel. At the entrance, he looked back over his shoulder. "You kin bunk in my room if you feel like," he called sullenly, then strode inside.

• • •

Evening. Avram sat on the edge of the wooden sidewalk, listening to the music from the Occidental Saloon across the street. After awhile he crossed to an alley at the side of the building and peered through a window into the bar.

It was a classy place. Huge mirrors hung from the walls between paintings of naked and half-naked ladies. There was a crystal chandelier. Gambling tables offered a choice of craps, faro, and monte. The music came from a banjo player, who strolled through the crowded saloon and took requests.

Avram started back across the street. An old man burst from a nearby door, wearing pink underwear and a bowler hat. He ran into the center of the street, doing a series of balletic leaps and springs.

"Yahoo!" he yelled. "Yaaaahooooo!"

Avram watched in silent amazement as the man continued down the middle of the thoroughfare, pirouetting and pivoting. What a wonderful country this is, thought Avram. You can be crazy, and still they don't lock you up. Without being aware of it, he began to mimic the dancing madman. He had almost made it back across the street when a voice stopped him short.

"Evening."

Avram looked up at a tin star that said "Sheriff" on it. The man wearing the star was a foot taller than Avram and eighty pounds heavier.

"Hello," said Avram.

"We don't allow dancing in the streets," said the sheriff. "You want to dance, go on over to the saloon."

"Thank you," said Avram. "Thank you."

The sheriff walked away, and Avram headed back toward the Occidental Saloon. He went inside, but remained near the door, somewhat overwhelmed by the sights and sounds. A honky-tonk piano was now adding its chords to those of the banjo. Waiters served mutton, grizzly bear, salmon, and the house specialty, canvasback duck. Available free was a punch made from red wine, white wine, champagne, and cognac. At the gaming tables, grizzled miners with five-hundred-dollars-a-night French prostitutes hanging all over them were placing bets, using bags of gold dust. A choking, smoky haze filled the entire room.

A voice caught Avram's attention. "Ain't I got the derndest luck."

Avram swung around and saw, standing near a roulette wheel—Matt Diggs. Darryll and Mr. Jones leaned over the table as the croupier paid off the bets.

"Woo-wee!" said Darryll. "You done it again, Matt!"

The croupier pushed a large pile of silver dollars in Matt's direction. Walking across the room, Avram spotted the silver plate engraved with the Ten Commandments hanging from Matt's neck. Without a word, he reached up and tore it loose, breaking the thin chain. Puzzled, Matt simply stared at him, trying to remember.

"What the hell you doing, mister?" said Darryll.

Avram took the plate to the piano player and placed it on top of the sheet music. "Would you hold this please?" he asked. Not waiting for a reply, he stalked back to Matt. "And now," he said, "I want my money back."

Jones looked at him sternly. "Who are you?"

"This fella's gotta be deranged," said Darryll. "Must be bad liquor. You been drinkin' that punch, maybe, mister? I heard that stuff can wreck a man's mind."

"I want my two hundred dollars," Avram told Matt.

"Piss off," said Matt. He gave Avram a shove, just hard enough to knock him off balance. He was quite surprised when Avram, regaining his footing, slammed a fist into his nose.

"Give it!" said Avram.

Matt touched his palm to his nostrils and looked in amazement at the thin ribbons of blood. There was a sudden hush in the saloon as people turned to stare; the music had stopped, and conversations were temporarily suspended.

"I don't want to hurt anybody," said Avram. "Just give me my money."

Matt regarded him calmly. "We're going to kill you," he said. He smashed his fist into the side of Avram's jaw, sending the rabbi reeling backward into a poker table. Avram sank to the floor alongside one of the players who spoke without taking his eyes off his cards. "Better stay on the floor, son. Pretend you're hurt serious."

The Diggs brothers were smiling; Darryll and Jones stood waiting just behind Matt. Avram climbed slowly to his feet, dusted himself off, then launched himself at the trio. Matt stood immobile until Avram was almost upon him, then feinted left, stepped to his right and tripped Avram with an outstretched foot. Avram fell forward directly onto Jones, who kneed him in the stomach and then lifted his face up by the beard.

"I'm warning you . . ." gasped Avram.

Jones smashed him in the right cheekbone, sending him flying into Darryll's outstretched arms. Darryll caught him, and with a shove of his foot returned him to Jones, who stopped Avram's forward motion with a fist in the face. Avram dropped to his knees, dazed. Jones again lifted him by the beard. Avram, on the way up, reached out frantically and felt his hand close on a beer mug that had been left on a nearby table. Before Jones could get off his next punch, Avram brought the mug up hard and heard the satisfying crunch of glass against skull. Jones's grip loosened, and Avram launched a flurry of weak punches at his face. Then Darryll picked up a chair and broke it over Avram's back.

"Oooh," said Avram, dropping again to his knees.

"Put him on the bar," said Matt.

Darryll and Jones lifted Avram and carried him across the room. They laid him on the bar lengthwise, face up. Matt lifted a wooden beer keg from one of the shelves and raised it high above Avram's face.

"I'm gonna smash his head to a pulp," he said.

He was just beginning the downward motion when a shot rang out. The keg sprung a gushing leak. Beer ran down over Matt's shirt. Moving forward from the door, pistol in hand, was Tommy Lillard.

"Don't anybody move," said Tommy.

The beer was drenching Matt's trousers.

"You . . ." continued Tommy, waving the gun at Jones, "put two hundred dollars on the bar."

Jones hesitated, glancing at Matt. Tommy's finger tightened on the trigger, and a bullet whizzed through the leather chaps on the inside of Jones's right thigh. Jones looked down in sick amazement.

"You know where the next one is goin'," said Tommy.

Jones backed cautiously to the roulette table, counted out a large amount of money, then returned quickly to lay it on the bar.

"You can put the barrel down," said Tommy to Matt, who still held the dripping keg raised above his head. Slowly, Matt lowered the keg to the floor. "Now," said Tommy, "I sugges' that all three of you . . . git the hell outa here afore I blows you up."

The three men walked wordlessly to the door and went out. Tommy holstered his gun and approached the bar, where Avram was just beginning to regain consciousness. Tommy poured someone's half-empty glass of beer over Avram's face.

"Wake up!"

Avram pulled himself to a sitting position.

"You're a rich man," said Tommy.

"Since when?"

"Since just now when you got your two hundred dollars back."

"I did?" said Avram.

"Yup."

"In that case, I would like a bath."

• • •

In the living room of the Bender home in San Francisco, Samuel Bender was shouting at his youngest daughter.

"You helped her!"

Rosalie, sewing, did not raise her eyes.

"You knew about it, and you knew it was going to happen."

Rosalie adjusted her thimble.

"Would you have the decency to answer me!" yelled Bender.

Rosalie put down the sewing and slowly raised her gaze. "I did help her."

"You helped her," echoed Bender sadly. "You helped your sister to break my heart. . . . Why?"

"When is your rabbi coming, Papa?"

"I DON'T KNOW!"

"That's right," said Rosalie. "You don't know. Maybe in a week, maybe in a year, maybe never."

"He's coming."

"Really, Papa? Are you so sure about everything that you're willing to bet your daughter's happiness?"

Bender stiffened. "You know—you know very well—that you and Sarah Mindl have always meant more to me than anything, anyone else. That I would give my life for you."

Rosalie nodded. "You love your daughters, but you don't really know us, Papa."

"I do—"

"I think you understand me a little, but Sarah is completely beyond you."

"How can you say that?"

"She wanted to please you," continued Rosalie, "but in my opinion, if she gave up Julius and waited for your rabbi, and he turned out to be a sack of potatoes who wanted to make love once every three months *if*—"

"Rosalie, please . . ."

"—*if* the moon was right, then I believe your daughter would have become a whore."

Bender turned away. "This kind of talk . . ."

"Is the truth, Papa. Maybe in the old country people spoke in riddles, or in circles, or didn't speak at all. But here . . . they say what's on their minds. It's better, Papa. Sometimes it hurts, but it's better."

Bender looked back determinedly. "All right. I'll tell you what's on my mind. I'm having a rabbi for a son-in-law. And if Sarah Mindl is gone, then he marries the next—and that's you."

Rosalie resumed her sewing. She raised her eyebrows coquettishly. "Yes . . . maybe . . . if I like his eyes, and I like his touch—"

"Must everything be a matter of biology?"

"—and if he likes me, and wants me, and he's not a sack of potatoes . . . it's possible."

Bender by this time was tugging at his hair. "Enough!" he shouted. "Enough! What is this world coming to!"

Rosalie, sewing away, would have told him if she thought he really wanted to know.

• • •

Climbing a low coastal hill, they passed a party of miners.

"Where you boys headed?" asked one of the men.

"San Francisco," said Avram. "And you?"

"Yuba River," said the man. "An if you was smart, you would too."

"Why's that?" asked Tommy.

"Ain't you heerd lump fever?" asked the miner. "Ever'body's got it. Other day, four greasers foun' a nugget up there weighed eight pounds."

Tommy grinned. "You b'lieve that?"

The miner dismissed him with a wave of the hand. "Crazy if you don't," he said.

Tommy laughed, and he and Avram continued on. As they crested the rise, they saw— the Pacific! "Damn!" said Tommy.

Avram dismounted and sank to his knees. "My God," he said. "My God." He prayed silently.

"You made it, Cuz," said Tommy.

"To me," said Avram, after his prayer, "this

227

is better than an eight-pound nugget. This is a twenty-pound nugget. A hundred-pound nugget."

Tommy shrugged. "Main reason this is better is 'cause it exists," he said. "Them other things don't."

They headed down toward the strip of narrow, sandy beach. Clumps of driftwood lay scattered near the high-water line, and there were a few large boulders near the bottom of the hill. Tommy managed to start a small fire, and then the two of them impulsively stripped off their clothes and plunged into the chill surf.

"It's frrrreeeezing!" yelled Avram, as he surfaced.

"Good for ya!" Tommy shouted back, diving into a wave.

Ten minutes later, numbed by the cold, they staggered out of the ocean and over the fine sand toward the mounds of piled clothing. Tommy used his flannel shirt to dry himself, then stood on one leg to slip on his pants. Playfully, Avram bumped him with a hip, knocking him lightly to the ground.

"Oh, I'm sorry," said Avram. "I didn't see you standing there."

He finished drying his body with Tommy's shirt and stepped into his own trousers.

Tommy, who had remained reclining in the sand, lunged at Avram's rear. "Here, lemme help you with those." He tugged Avram's pants down to his knees, spilling the rabbi backward. "I hate a crowded beach," he said. Avram leaped at him, and they began to wrestle, rolling over and over, laughing, trying to pin each other's shoulders. Suddenly a shot rang out, and a bullet thudded into the sand an inch from Tommy's foot.

Avram and Tommy disengaged, as the Diggs brothers and Mr. Jones rode slowly toward them, Darryll carrying a pistol, Matt and Jones double-barreled shotguns.

Tommy glanced helplessly at his own holstered handguns, six feet away.

The men on horseback walked their mounts slowly forward. Matt, spotting the Torah between two saddles in front of the smoldering fire, reached down with his shotgun and nudged the scrolls into the glowing ashes. Avram felt his Adam's apple swell up in his throat.

"Let's get on with it," said Matt solemnly.

"Let me," said Jones. But as he raised his shotgun, Tommy grabbed Avram by the back of the neck, thrust him forcefully to the ground, then dived into the sand and somehow, miraculously, scratching and rolling, came up with one of his own holstered guns. Jones was able to get off one shot before Tommy, firing without taking the gun from its sheath, put a bullet dead center in his forehead. Jones pitched slowly forward, a cadaver before he hit the ground. Matt's horse, startled by the gunfire, reared in panic, causing Matt's shot to go wild. Darryll, who had dismounted, fired one at Tommy, even though he was running backward to take cover behind a driftwood log.

The Torah burst into flames. Scrambling toward the ashes, Avram managed to grab the handle of one of the scrolls and lift the Torah out onto the sand where he tried to smother the fire. Meanwhile Tommy, who had fired once at Darryll and missed, fired again at Matt and grazed his right eyebrow. Matt dropped his pistol in the sand and clutched at his right eye with both hands. Blood spurted through his fingers as his horse carried him toward the nearby boulders. From behind the driftwood, Darryll continued to peg shots at Tommy.

"Get the gun!" Tommy screamed to Avram. "He dropped his gun! Over there!"

Avram beat the burning Torah into the sand.

"Get the gun, fer Chrissake!" yelled Tommy again. "Help me!" He looked around frantically, but the nearest cover was twenty feet away.

Avram put down the Torah, the flames finally extinguished. Tommy, backing away, saw the barrel of Darryll's pistol come up over the driftwood, pause, and track his movement. He tried to change direction—too late. The bullet caught him high in the left chest, just below the shoulder. The impact sent him stumbling sideways and back, his gun dropping in the sand, where Avram retrieved it. Darryll stood up, took careful aim, and fired. A click—nothing happened. Once more he sighted on Tommy's prostrate form, squeezed the trigger—and again, nothing. His gun was empty.

Avram held Tommy's pistol awkwardly in his hand.

"Shoot him!" gasped Tommy.

Avram looked back at Darryll and hesitated. Darryll spotted Jones's shotgun, lying next to his body. He watched as Avram took aim, saw the look on his face, the quivering of his hand. Slowly, deliberately, his eyes always on Avram, Darryll walked to Jones's body and picked up the shotgun. Avram was shaking and shivering all over.

"Shoot!" pleaded Tommy. "Shoot him! He's gonna kill us!"

Avram willed his arm to stop shaking, commanded the muscles in his hand to steady. Darryll raised the shotgun carefully to his shoulder, aimed at Avram's head—and was quite surprised when he saw Avram's finger tighten on the trigger. He died with the astonishment still on his face, and a huge, wine-red stain spreading rapidly over his shirt.

Avram dropped the pistol and ran over to Tommy.

"Glad you didn' wait too much longer," said Tommy weakly. "Woulda spoiled the endin'."

Gently, Avram used a handkerchief to wipe some of the blood from Tommy's wound. He felt dazed by the suddenness of the attack and the extreme violence. "Are you in much pain?" he asked.

"Jus' looks bad, Cuz. I been hurt a lot worse than this afore." Tommy winced. "Can you check to see if the slug's still in me?"

"How . . . how do I . . . ?"

"Jus' raise me up a bit."

Avram helped Tommy to a half-sitting posture.

"Now check my back."

Avram looked behind Tommy's shoulder and saw a gaping, bloody hole. "Ripped open," he said.

"Good!" said Tommy, clenching his teeth.

"Mus' be my lucky day. Bullet pass right through."

"I still . . . " said Avram. "Tell me what . . . "

"Git the whiskey from my bedroll. An' bring my saddle pouch."

"I have no expérience in these things," said Avram.

"Don' need none," said Tommy. "Simple as shit. You git the stuff, I'll show ya how to fix me. Okay?"

Avram nodded, but did not move.

Tommy looked at him carefully. "You never killed a man before, did ya?"

Avram stared into the distance.

"Listen to me," continued Tommy. "You had to, or we'd both be dead."

Avram compressed his lips.

"If I forgit to tell ya later on," said Tommy, "or if I pass out for a little while . . . you remember to check the horses, right?"

"Yes."

"You'll see that they're okay?"

"Yes."

"An' watch out to make sure that the guy that got away—the one I grazed over the eye— watch he don' come back. I doubt he will, but you watch anyways." Tommy sank back in the sand.

"I will." Avram stood up.

"Now git the whiskey."

Avram fetched two bottles from Tommy's bedroll. He gave one to Tommy, who drank as he spoke.

"Now you do 'xactly what I say, an' ever'-

thin' be all right. Git a shirt an' tear it inta strips."

Avram took one of his own undershirts and tore it up.

"That gonna be the bandages," said Tommy, wiping his lips. "Now, take th' other bottle an' pour the whiskey in my wound."

"But—"

"Do it."

Avram dripped the liquid into the still-bleeding bullet hole.

Tommy closed his eyes. "More! Really shake it in there."

Avram thoroughly soaked the mutilated flesh as Tommy grunted in pain.

"Now go git a twig from the fire. Make sure it's still lit."

"Look, I don't think—"

"You want me to go on livin'?"

"Of course, but I—"

"Then do as I say!" yelled Tommy.

Avram fetched a stick from the flames, its tip still burning.

"Now," said Tommy, "you touch the twig to my wounds, front an' back. When it's done, you give it 'bout two minutes, then smother it an' put on them bandages." He drained his bottle and looked up. "Don' be scared," he said softly. "It ain' nothin'."

Closing his eyes, he gave one quick nod. Avram, fighting off waves of nausea, touched the stick twice to the alcohol-soaked wounds, then retched as they burst into flames. Tommy screamed, a high-pitched shriek of agony. His body twitched and jerked, groups of muscles contracting uncontrollably. Twenty seconds later, he passed into unconsciousness.

It was night time when Tommy awoke. He sat up slowly and saw Avram bending over the fire. Gingerly, he probed his shoulder. He was dressed in a shirt, and he could feel the make-shift bandages under his sleeves and across his chest. The wound was completely numb now, and there were no signs of bleeding.

"Hey," he called.

Avram looked around. "Oh, thank God," he said. "You're up. A miracle. Thank God."

"Gave you a hard time, huh?" said Tommy.

Avram brought over some biscuits and a cup of coffee. He ran his hand through Tommy's hair. "You are in great pain?"

"Nope. Not anymore. Tomorrow she'll start to throb, but the worst is over. If I ain't got fever now, I'll heal fine." He wolfed down one of the biscuits. "You had a rough go, huh?"

"Not like you," said Avram. "For me it was nothing . . . "

"Never you mind," said Tommy. "'Less you're one of them there sadists, there's a lot more pleasant work aroun'." He paused. "Worst thing is the smell, ain't it? The charred skin."

Avram nodded.

"You done fine," said Tommy. "Real fine."

Avram returned to the fire. "Would you like some more coffee?"

"No."

"I think maybe you should try and sleep then."

234

"If'n you say so, Doc." Tommy chuckled.

Avram lugged over one of the saddles, bunched his coat on top of it, and placed the makeshift pillow gently under Tommy's head.

"You'd be a good wife," said Tommy. "You know that?"

"Well," said Avram, "when you're ready to make a formal proposal, we'll talk business." He went back to the fire.

Tommy studied him from the distance. "You okay?" he asked.

"Me?" said Avram. "I'm fine."

"You been actin' . . . I dunno, funny-like."

"*I've* been acting funny? You've been unconscious, you're someone to talk."

"I mean, you jus' . . . you don' seem happy like you always do. You sure you're all right?"

"Yes!" said Avram sharply. "Go to sleep!"

Tommy turned on his side. "Hey, Rabbi," he said, "you think God sent me to show you the way?"

"What's the difference what I think?"

"Do ya?"

"Perhaps. Who knows?" Avram stared out at the rolling waves of water, black swells crashing on the beach in the dim light from the stars. His coffee had grown cold in his tin cup.

"I must be some kin' of a fuckin' angel," said Tommy groggily. He yawned. "Goddamn if that ain't what I am."

(13)

The next day, late in the afternoon in a light rain, Tommy and Avram rode into San Francisco. The town's growth, in just the past few months, had gone from wild to explosive. Each day there were thirty new houses, two murders and a fire. Top prostitutes earned fifty thousand dollars a year. There were one thousand gambling halls; interest rates on loans to losers were ten percent—per hour. In the harbor, the masts of docked ships formed a cluster thicker than the densest forest. The town's rat population increased even faster than the human; stray cats sold for ten dollars apiece.

Tommy and Avram stopped in Portsmouth Square, formerly a potato patch, but now a hotel, gambling and restaurant center.

Tommy pointed to the El Dorado Casino. "I'll be in there when you're through with your business."

Avram nodded and headed his horse away.

"You know where you're goin'?" called Tommy.

"DuPont Street," said Avram. "It's right nearby."

"You take care now," called Tommy. "Lotta bad folks roun' here. Keep away from Sydney Town."

Avram waved.

Five minutes later, the Torah cradled in his arms, a piece of paper with a penciled address in one hand, he stood outside the Bender residence in the fading light. He stepped up onto the wooden porch and laid the Torah carefully against the crack in the door, upright so that it could not fail to be noticed. As he straightened up, however, the door opened abruptly and he found himself face to face with a lovely young lady. It was Rosalie, he recognized her from the photograph.

"Oy!" he exclaimed.

"Yes?" said Rosalie.

Avram touched his hand to his hat. "Oh, uh, howdy there, ma'am."

Rosalie looked at him strangely. "Do you want something?"

"Gol dang it," said Avram, "yes, ah do, ma'am. M' name is Tommy Lillard, an' ah come from the Texas, uh, from . . . from Texas."

"Funny," Rosalie said. "You don't look like you come from Texas."

"Well, ah do ma'am," said Avram, "an'

238

ah'm right sorry if'n ah gave you a *bissel*, ah mean a little . . . a little startle there. Ah was a might startled mahself there for a second."

"I still don't know what it is you want," said Rosalie suspiciously.

"Oh," said Avram, lifting up the Torah. "Well, this here thang is fer Mr. Bender, if'n ah got the right house an' all."

Rosalie continued to gaze at him, at the black hat and curly sideburns particularly, and the white hands, and the face . . . a certain softness, sensitivity. "You do have the right house," she said. "I'm Mr. Bender's daughter."

"Oh. Howdy, ma'am."

"Would you care to come in?"

"Well, ah'd like to, ma'am, but—"

"Please."

"No, no, ah'd better not. See, mah friend, the rabbi—well, he give me this here thang an' tol' me jus' to brang it over to Mr. Bender, an' uh—"

"What *is* it?" asked Rosalie, staring.

"Well, ah don't rightly know, miss. Religious type thang of some sort."

"You mean you don't know what it is that you're delivering?"

"Ah b'lieve he called it a 'Toree', ma'am."

"A toree? What's a toree?" Her face brightened. "You mean a Torah?"

"Thass it!" said Avram. "A Torah. Thass exac'ly what he said it vass, uh . . . was."

"Where is he?"

"Who?"

"The rabbi."

"What rabbi?"

239

"The one you—"

"Oh, the rabbi! Well, he . . . don't rightly know, m'am. Las' time ah seed him ah was bustin' mah britches in a, a . . . cat's house, an'—"

"Where?"

"A cat house," said Avram quickly. "I meant . . . Anyway, this here rabbi come along an' asked me if'n ah should ever pass near 'Frisco, would ah do this for him."

Rosalie nodded slowly. "Uh huh, uh huh . . ." She looked at Avram's face, observed his dazed expression.

"Well," said Avram, "m' friend is waitin' at the saloon. Ah gotta, you know, mosey right along now an' . . ."

"Is something wrong?"

Avram, overwhelmed by her beauty, fought to keep from stuttering. "Well, uh, no. No. It's just, uh . . . God, I . . . I didn't realize that your eyes would be quite so big, so—"

"How would you know that?" asked Rosalie.

"I wouldn't," said Avram quickly. "I wouldn't know that. It was a guess."

Rosalie tilted her head. "You guessed I would have big eyes?"

"I'm a terrific guesser," said Avram. "A regular guessin' fool, mah friends say." He stepped off the porch. "Well, ah gotta be goin' now, ma'am. Hate to keep mah sidewinder standin' there—"

"Wait!" said Rosalie. "Please!" She turned back inside. "Papa!" she yelled. "Papa!"

Avram backed quickly away. "Adios, m'am."

"Wait!" called Rosalie as he disappeared into the darkness. "Wait, please . . ."

· · ·

Avram stared listlessly at the tray of salmon and potatoes before him. The El Dorado was similar to the Occidental Saloon in San Jose, except everything—area, furnishings, women— was scaled up ten times. Food was free to encourage gambling. French, German, Chinese and Mexican dishes were readily available. The primary card game was monte; it took too long to win or lose money at poker. Instead of a piano and banjo, the El Dorado featured a string quartet and strolling violinists. Queen Charlottes, mixtures of wine and raspberry syrup, were offered without charge to all women; "stone fences"—whiskey and cider—were provided for the men.

Tommy stuffed himself with steak. He glanced over at Avram to see if he had drunk any beer from the mug before him. He hadn't. Tommy reached over, speared one of Avram's potatoes with his fork, and downed it quickly with a piece of meat. "If you don't eat your food, then I will," he said.

"Be my guest," said Avram.

"Never you mind," said Tommy. "You jus' eat. Then we'll go together, an' you tell your people that their new rabbi has arrived." He stopped chewing. "All right?"

"I can't be a rabbi," said Avram quietly.

Tommy flung his fork on the table. "Don't say that again! Now jus' don't say it!"

"So I won't say it."

"Damn right, you won't. Not after what

I've been through to git your goddamn ass here alive."

Avram closed his eyes and nodded.

"If you hadn't shot that man," said Tommy fiercely, "we'd both be dead! Do you unnerstan' that, you ignorant asshole?"

Avram nodded again.

"You *do* unnerstan' that."

"Yes."

"He was goin' to kill you. And then he was goin' to kill me. Am I right?"

"Yes."

"Is there somethin' in the Jew religion says a man can't defend hisself from someone tryin' to kill him?"

"No."

"So when you shot that sonofabitch, *that was not a sin.*"

Avram nodded.

"Then what the hell are we talkin' about?" Tommy slapped the table in exasperation.

Avram's face twisted in pain. "When those men were shooting at you . . . I ran to save the Torah."

"Well, there you are!" said Tommy. "That proves it. I unnerstan' that. Any fool unnerstan's that. You're a man of God. There you are."

"I did not do it because of God."

"Huh?"

"I wasn't thinking about God! I don't understand one word about God!" Avram was shouting now, his face red, his eyes filled with tears. "I was thinking about a book."

"Aw—"

242

"I cared more for the book than I did for you," Avram said sadly.

"The book is holy. The book—"

"There is nothing so holy as the life of a human being," said Avram. "I don't want to insult you, but do you understand what I'm saying? I chose a piece of parchment instead of you."

"I forgive you!"

"I know."

"It was no big deal . . ."

"It was a very big deal," contradicted Avram.

"But you're a good man . . ."

Avram nodded. "I *am* a good man. But a rabbi is more. He is learned and wise and just." He hesitated. "I am not a rabbi."

"Don't say that!"

"I'm not a—"

Tommy snatched up the mug of beer and dashed the liquid in Avram's face. "Damn!" he shouted. He grabbed the front of Avram's shirt. "DON'T SAY THAT TO ME! You are a rabbi! I am a bank robber. I am a card player and whoremonger. Thass who I am. You are a rabbi."

Avram wiped the beer from his eyes. "I could think more clearly if you released my shirt," he said.

Tommy let go of him. "You're a rabbi," he repeated. "You can fall on your ass an' slip in the mud an' travel in the wrong direction, but even on your ass, even in the mud, even in the wrong direction . . . you're still a rabbi." He paused. "You are who you are," he said softly.

Avram looked at his friend with new respect. "Perhaps . . . you are correct," he said hesitantly.

"No perhaps about it," said Tommy. "If I'm

who I am, then how come you ain't who you are?" His eyes narrowed. "Or are you jus' too goddammed good to have the same rules?"

Avram bowed his head. "No," he said. "I'm not too good—" From the corner of his eye, he saw a small group of people approach, then halt five feet from the table. Beer still dripped from his beard.

Rosalie and her father stepped forward from the delegation. Bialik, Rosensheine and their families remained at a respectful distance.

"Excuse me," said Mr. Bender to Tommy. "My name is Samuel Bender, President of the Congregation Beth Israel. Are you the rabbi?"

"Huh?" said Tommy.

Bender switched to Yiddish. "I was told that our new rabbi had arrived. Is that you?"

Tommy looked at Avram. "What's he talkin' 'bout?"

"He wants to know if you're the rabbi," translated Avram.

"Me?"

"Yes."

"Tommy shrugged. "Tell him."

Avram stared at Rosalie and then at Bender. "*I'm* the rabbi," he said finally.

Bender's eyes widened. "You? You're the rabbi?"

"You've never seen a rabbi before, maybe?" said Avram.

"But . . . but what are you doing in here? This place?"

"I've just crossed three thousand miles, and I was thanking my dear friend for getting me here alive."

"This man is your friend?" said Bender, drawing back to gaze again at Tommy.

"My name," said Avram, "is Avram Mutz, and don't judge people by their appearance."

"We have a rabbi!" shouted Mr. Bialik.

"A rabbi!" echoed someone in the crowd.

"Tenk Got!"

"*Kinehora.*"

"*Mazel Tov!*"

Bender and Bialik shook hands. Mrs. Rosensheine hugged Avram tightly around the chest.

At last Bender loudly cleared his throat. "I'm sorry, Rabbi," he said formally. "Forgive me, please."

"Of course," said Avram.

"I am very, very happy to see you," continued Bender. "Let's have some schnaps!"

"I'll git the booze," said Tommy, heading for the bar.

Bender tugged on Avram's sleeve. "Rabbi," he said, "this is my youngest daughter, Rosalie." He put his hand on Rosalie's back.

Avram smiled shyly.

"I know," continued Bender, "that in our marriage agreement I mentioned my other daughter, Sarah Mindl, but what difference—"

"Papa!" said Rosalie, blushing.

Bender seemed flustered, momentarily but then, increasing the pressure on Rosalie's back, he said, "What's the matter with you? Say hello to the rabbi."

Rosalie gave Avram a swift, significant look. "Hello, Rabbi. I'm very pleased to meet you."

Avram, delighted that she had kept their little secret, said, "I'm very pleased to meet you."

245

Bender stared at Avram's beard. "Some more beer, Rabbi?"

"Yes, that would be fine," said Avram.

"I'll find your friend at the bar," said Bender, and made his way through the crowd. A moment later he was addressing a mustachioed bartender. "A beer, please. Make it a large one." He spotted Tommy a few feet away. "And you, my friend, may I buy you some whiskey?"

Tommy held up a bottle. "Jus' got this 'un fer the crowd. Help yourself." He signaled another bartender for two glasses.

"Thank you very much," said Bender.

"Mah pleasure," said Tommy.

"Tell me," said Bender, "are you Orthodox or Conservative?" He watched as Tommy filled his glass.

"Well, I certainly ain't conservative" said Tommy. He raised his glass. "Here's to gittin' laid."

"To . . . happy days," said Bender uncertainly, lifting his own glass.

As Tommy slugged down his drink, his elbow brushed a massive shoulder next to him. "Sorry," he said. " 'Scuse me."

Bender accepted his beer from the bartender and started back toward Avram. The owner of the massive shoulder turned to face Tommy.

"That's all right," said Matt Diggs.

Before Tommy could react, Matt had cradled his head in one huge hand and smashed it down on the bar, the concussion immediately rendering Tommy unconscious. As several men turned to stare, Matt propped Tommy's body up against a stool.

"Hold on there, fella," he said loudly. "You better just sleep it off." Smiling he made his way through the tables until he reached Avram. "'Scuse me, Rabbi," he said, pushing past Rosensheine, Bialik and the others.

Avram looked up and felt the blood drain from his face. "Yes?"

"Beggin' yer pardon, Rabbi. I'd like to talk to ya for a moment."

Avram excused himself from the table. He and Diggs moved a few feet away.

"I am glad that you are alive," said Avram.

"I'll bet," said Diggs.

"I am," said Avram.

"I'm sure you are. I'm gonna kill you."

Avram shook his head. "Look, please, no more trouble. Haven't we hurt each other enough? Can't there be an end to the bloodshed?"

"Sure can," said Diggs. "Right after I blow a hole in you big enough to drive a train through."

"There are laws—"

"It's all gonna be strictly legal," said Diggs. "I'm not gonna hang for it, an' I'm not gonna go to jail. You an' me'll have a fair fight, with you endin' up dead."

"How can it be fair unless we both—"

"Shut yer mouth! I want you outside—now!"

Avram clenched his teeth. "No . . . more . . . killing."

"Oh, yes," said Matt, his face contorted with rage. "Oh, yes."

"Please," pleaded Avram. "I don't want more violence. Don't do this, please."

247

"Outside," said Matt. "Right now. Yella-belly."

Avram stood firm. "I'm not afraid to die," he said quietly, "but I don't want you to kill ... and I don't want to kill."

"Don't worry none 'bout that las' part," said Diggs. He stepped in front of Rosalie. "L'il dance, ma'am?"

Rosalie, not perceiving the menace, smiled sweetly. Matt took her in his arms, and then began to dance to the music of a strolling vio-linist. "Ain't this a cute l'il thing?" he said, cir-cling near Avram.

Avram kept silent, afraid of alarming Rosa-lie. He hoped that somehow the situation would be defused.

"Pretty girl," said Diggs, hugging Rosalie tighter. "You know, there's lots of pretty girls here tonight, but I don't know—there's just some-thin' 'bout this partic'lar one I really hanker after."

Avram wondered if Matt somehow knew about his and Rosalie's special relationship—or whether Matt's dancing with her was just an unfortunate coincidence.

"You think it's 'cause she got such big eyes?" said Matt loudly.

The question was answered. Avram's heart sank. Diggs had been spying on him from the moment he had entered San Francisco, had probably tracked him and Tommy since the shootout at the beach.

"I'll tell ya," offered Matt, "maybe not to-night, maybe not tomorry, but I'm gonna have me this girl." He reached around and pinched Rosalie's behind.

Rosalie gave a little squeal of surprise and pulled away.

"Well . . .?" said Matt, giving Avram a challenging stare.

Avram hesitated, then nodded reluctantly.

Matt bounded up onto the table. "Hey!" he yelled. "Everybody! Hey, listen up . . ."

Heads turned.

"Stop playing a minute!" shouted Matt to the string quartet.

Abruptly, there was silence. Dealers, croupiers, gamblers, drinkers—all turned to look at Matt. "You!" Matt yelled, addressing the head bartender. "You listenin' to me?"

The man nodded.

"This here fella killed mah brother." Matt thrust a thumb toward Avram. "We're gonna have a fair fight. There ain't no advantage being taken here."

Matt looked around to gauge the effect of his words. It was important that he be believed. The Committee of Vigilance, as they called themselves, had summarily hanged more than one man from the beams of their headquarters on Battery Street.

"He's agreed to fight me," Matt went on. "We're goin' outside so's no innocent people get hurt."

"What is this?" murmured Bender. "What is he talking?"

"I jus' want it down for the record," said Matt. "This is a fair fight."

The bartender wiped off a glass. "Is what he says true?" he asked Avram.

Avram said nothing.

"Is it?" persisted the bartender. "Did you kill his brother an' now you're fightin' him fair an' square?"

Avram nodded.

"All right, then," said the bartender. "Outside, both of you!"

Matt jumped off the table, and Avram started toward the door. There was a confused clamor of Yiddish and English as people pushed their way outside.

In the street, Matt shoved a pistol into Avram's right hand. "There ya go! Jus' like a man."

Avram held the gun limply.

Matt began to back away. "Don't worry," he called. "That's the gun you used before when you killed my brother Darryll."

"Please . . ."

"Don't wanna take no advantage, now."

They were in the middle of the street, thirty feet apart, with curious crowds lining both sidewalks. Matt's hand dangled ominously near his holster. The crowd hushed.

"Make your move," snarled Matt.

Avram stood motionless.

"You got the advantage!"

"Look, please, let's—"

"Make your move!"

Avram shook his head.

Deliberately, Matt drew his gun, aimed, and fired. The bullet chipped Avram on the left arm, tearing his shirt but barely touching the flesh.

"Draw!"

Avram did not respond.

Again, Matt squeezed the trigger. This time the bullet hit flesh, lower on the same arm. A red blotch spread on Avram's sleeve.

"Stop it!" screamed Rosalie, horrified. She lurched forward, but was immediately restrained by four men. "He'll kill him," she wailed.

"There's nothing we can do," said Bialik.

"You could help him!"

"We can't. It's a fair fight."

"Fair? You call this fair? It's murder, it's—"

Bender hugged her to his chest. "It's in God's hands, *bubeleh*."

Matt was in a rage. "You skunk. You yella, lily-livered coward! You're gonna shoot that gun, or you're gonna die."

Avram shrugged.

"Ain't no one gonna say I didn't give you a fair fight." Matt glanced around at the crowd. "I'm gonna count to three . . . you hear me?"

Avram gave no sign of acknowledgment. What a shame, he thought. To make it all that distance, and then to die like this. He considered turning his back, forcing his enemy to shoot him from behind, but found himself paralyzed, unable to move. What's the difference? he thought. Back or front, I'm equally defenseless.

"To three!" repeated Matt. "An' then I shoot. You do whatever you think best." He paused. "One!"

The killer and the about-to-be-killed stared at each other.

"Two!" came a voice from the sidewalk.

Matt turned and saw Tommy coming forward. Tommy positioned himself between Matt and Avram. "This ain't your fight!" Matt yelled.

"I'm makin' it mah fight," said Tommy. Eyeing Matt steadily, he walked two steps closer.

"That Jew killed my brother!" Matt yelled.

Tommy clicked his tongue in mock sympathy. "You an' your pig-faced brother an' your weasel partner ambushed us on that beach."

"Because you and the Jew took our two hundred dollars!"

"Which you stole from mah friend in the first place," Tommy said.

Matt shuffled his feet. "Stealin' ain't the same as killin'. He killed mah kinfolk."

"An' if he hadn't, it'd be us that'd be dead by now," said Tommy. "I believe the count is two," he added coolly.

Avram saw Matt's expression turn to panic. He realized a distressing thing; Matt was as mismatched and helpless against Tommy as he himself was against Matt. "Don't kill him!" he yelled impulsively to Tommy.

At this, sensing the only advantage he would ever have, Matt drew—but not fast enough. In a blur of motion, Tommy drew his own gun and shot the pistol out of Matt's hand. Shouting incoherently, Matt charged at Avram, drawing a knife as he ran. Avram stood unmoving and let his gun drop to the ground.

"You sonofabitch gutless Jew coward!" shrieked Matt. Two yards from Avram, he raised his knife to strike.

At the last instant, in a move very similar to

one Matt had used on him before, Avram feinted to his left and stepped to his right, extending his left foot for Matt to trip over. Matt fell heavily, but recovered fast, rolling over. Avram plunged down on top of him, crashing the point of his elbow into Matt's jaw. Quickly, Avram drew the blade given to him by Natimucca.

"You think," he gasped, "you think you're the only one with a knife?"

He thrust the point of the blade powerfully through the leather of Matt's jacket sleeve, pinning Matt to the ground.

"No more killing," said Avram. "No more."

He stood up, breathing heavily. He saw the crowd beginning to close in, Tommy out in front.

Tommy touched a hand to his own cheek. *"Veh iz mir!"* he said.

• • •

It was, to say the least, a strange affair.

Since there was no rabbi to marry the rabbi, Mr. Bialik read Rosalie and Avram the wedding vows. Since the synagogue was too small to accommodate all the guests, the reception was held in the El Dorado. Although the congregation was presumably Orthodox, the bride refused to have her hair shorn before the ceremony and would not look at the expensive *shaytl*—wig—her father had bought for her. There was not even a *nadan*, because she did not believe in a dowry. "He is marrying me because he loves me, not because he wants my family's money," was her position.

And so, what was left was the breaking of

the wine glass, a shower of barley grains, and a hen and a rooster, for fertility, preceding the couple as they walked from the synagogue to the El Dorado.

"What a wonderful life!" marveled Avram to Rosalie, after the *motzi* had been said over the *choleh*. "I've crossed rivers, climbed mountains, was captured by wonderful Indians . . . God has truly blessed me."

Rosalie was about to respond when Tommy cut between them and gave the bride a lingering kiss.

"And what's more," said Avram to no one in particular, "how many rabbis can say that they had a bank robber for a best man?"

BESTSELLING BOOKS OF MOVIE HITS
FROM WARNER...

E GOODBYE GIRL
Robert Grossbach (89-556, $1.95)
ula had a weakness for big, handsome, macho actors.
t the man who was dripping water on her rug and
nted to share her apartment was short and wore
isses so there would be no problems of the heart. A
lightful love story of New York and its theatre.

LIFORNIA SUITE
Robert Grossbach (90-006, $1.95)
vesdrop at the Beverly Hills Hotel. On the Barries who
e there to pick up an Oscar. On the two doctors who
nt to play tennis without their wives. On Hannah who's
from New York to pick up a runaway daughter. On
arvin, who doesn't really know why he's there. The
nniest novel of the year!

E CHEAP DETECTIVE
Robert Grossbach (89-557, $1.95)
knows every cheap trick, cheap joke, cheap shot and
eap dame in the book. Could that be why six females
ep chasing him as he chases down the clues in the
ost murderously funny book since *Murder By Death*?
is is murder by the case, laughter by the barrelful, all
livered by Neil Simon's Cheap Detective!

E BRINK'S JOB
Noel Behn (91-108, $2.50)
med men in Captain Marvel masks. A robbery six years
the planning and total chaos in the execution. Here's
e dramatic, true "you-are-there" story of the fabulous
,700,000 Brink's robbery — as seen by the men who
d it. One of the best books about criminals ever
itten!

PERMAN: LAST SON OF KRYPTON
Elliot S. Maggin (82-319, $2.25)
the dying planet Krypton tears itself apart, Jor-El,
ypton's greatest scientist, launches a tiny interstellar
p into the frigid void of space bearing in its hold his
ly child — the infant who will become Earth's Super-
an! From his childhood in Smallville, to his emergence
Metropolis newsman Clark Kent, through his battles
th his arch-enemy Lex Luthor, his story is told anew
d as never before, with all the high drama and excite-
ent that have enthralled three generations of fans!

BEST OF BESTSELLERS
FROM WARNER...

WITHOUT FEATHERS
by Woody Allen (89-035, $1.95)

"If you want to read the funniest book of the year, and don't care
if you break into helpless whoops of laughter on buses, trains
or wherever you happen to be reading it, get hold of WITHOUT
FEATHERS." —*Chicago Tribune Book World*

THE BUSHWHACKED PIANO
by Thomas McGuane (89-477, $1.95)

A delightfully insane novel about a bona-fide American hero tool-
ing across the country in pursuit of an equally lunatic heiress.
It's coast to coast laughs with a lot of wisdom inbetween. "A
wild, raunchy, funny dirty comedy about the American Male."
—*Publishers Weekly*

THE COMPLETE UNABRIDGED SUPER TRIVIA ENCYCLOPEDIA
by Fred L. Worth (83-882, $2.95)

864 pages of pure entertainment. A panoply of sports, movies,
comics, television, radio, rock 'n' roll, you-name-it, at your finger
tips. The biggest, the best, the most comprehensive trivia book
ever created!

WARNER BOOKS
P.O. Box 690
New York, N.Y. 10019

Please send me the books I have selected.

Enclose check or money order only, no cash
please. Plus 50¢ per order and 10¢ per copy
to cover postage and handling. N.Y. State and
California residents add applicable sales tax.

Please allow 4 weeks for delivery.

_____ Please send me your free
mail order catalog

Name_____

Address_____

City_____

State_____ Zip_____